Ride
Away
Home

Ride Away Home

WILLIAM WELLS

THE PERMANENT PRESS
Sag Harbor, NY 11963

For information, address:
  The Permanent Press
  4170 Noyac Road
  Sag Harbor, NY 11963
  www.thepermanentpress.com

Library of Congress Cataloging-in-Publication Data

Wells, William—
  Ride away home / William Wells.
    pages cm
  ISBN 978-1-57962-359-3
    1. Fathers and daughters—Fiction. 2. Children—Death—
  Psychological aspects—Fiction. 3. Children of the rich—Fiction.
  4. Bereavement—Fiction. I. Title.

PS3623.E4795R53 2014
813'.6—dc23   2014014218

Printed in the United States of America

For our grandson Jack Ambrose Wells,
brand-new to our world.

ACKNOWLEDGMENTS

Martin and Judith Shepard, co-owners of The Permanent Press of Sag Harbor, New York, took my submitted manuscript on a vacation to Morocco. When they returned, they called me, both on the line, told me how much they liked Ride Away Home, and that they wanted to publish it. If there is a nicer phone call for a writer to get, I don't know what it might be. The Permanent Press is a safe harbor for writers in the stormy seas of today's book publishing world, and I am both honored and grateful to be on their list.

Judith improved the book with her editorial suggestions, as did copy editor Barbara Anderson, who saved me from committing errors of spelling, grammar and logic. Lon Kirschner, who is a motorcycle man himself, did an excellent cover design.

I am indebted to friends who were first readers of this novel and who offered both encouragement and helpful suggestions for improvements.

Finally, and most importantly, even though I'd started and stopped several novels over the years without finishing them, my wife Mary continued to offer support and encouragement for my writing, even when there was no apparent reason for her to do so. Every writer should be so lucky.

"In the middle of the journey of our life
I came to myself within a dark wood
where the straight way was lost."

—Dante Alighieri, *"The Inferno"*

1

I've driven this stretch of I-94, which runs east and west across the broad belly of Wisconsin's black-loamed farmland, countless times over the years. But never before on a motorcycle. And not just any motorcycle, but a brand-new Harley-Davidson Road King Classic with a "hard candy lucky green flake" custom paint job, as the manufacturer calls the color.

It's a real beast of a machine that I'm riding for the first time, except for a training session in the dealer's parking lot in Minneapolis that lasted less than an hour, not nearly enough time to build any level of confidence in my two-wheel ability.

When I started and revved the Harley's engine in my garage early this morning, I flinched at the loud, percussive explosion of valves and pistons coming suddenly to life as the noise reverberated off the garage walls: VROOOM! VROOOM! VROOOM! Until then, I'd only heard the engine run outside—the difference between a jungle cat's roar in your living room and in the wild. Two kids from the Harley dealership trucked my new motorcycle to my house three days ago and pushed it into the garage. I've had a lot to do preparing for this trip, including going to the DMV to get my motorcycle license learner's permit, so the cycle remained there, idle until this morning.

I powered the cycle out of the garage, feeding it too much gas at first, in danger of being bucked off, then panic-stopped, and closed the overhead door with a remote, which I stowed in the glove compartment. Yes, the Harley has a glove compartment, as well as antilock brakes, cruise control, GPS, and a Bose stereo system with Bluetooth headphones: the full tilt boogie, cycle-wise. There is some other stuff too, which I'll learn about when I take the time to read the owner's manual. For now, it's in my saddlebags, still in its shrink wrap.

As I eased down my driveway and into the street at seven A.M., I felt as if I'd had a brief ground school session and was now taxiing along a runway for my first solo airplane flight. My neighbor, Stan Delahaye, collecting his newspaper on his front porch, gave me a curious look and a wave. Stan is an orthopedic surgeon at the Hennepin County Medical Center, so maybe he was thinking: *see you in my OR, Jack.* I was too nervous to take a hand off the grip to return Stan's wave, so I just nodded my head at him.

As the Harley and I made our way slowly through my neighborhood, turning heads and causing dogs to bark, I wouldn't have minded if my new motorcycle came with training wheels like my first bicycle, at least until I got more comfortable with the whole affair, whenever that would be. But training wheels are one of the few options the Harley-Davidson Motor Company does not offer. So I'll either improve en route, or not.

But this is a trip I have to make, or at least attempt to make, even though it's a very chilly March 1, and I've come this far, two hours from home now on the beginning of a very long ride. Fortunately, the Alberta Clippers that brought snow and subzero temperatures to the Upper Midwest for much of the winter have subsided, at least for a while, and I have a window of relative warmth, 30s and 40s, and dry roads, as I head south to a warmer climate.

I'VE BEEN gradually adding speed as cars and trucks whoosh past me, at first just trying to stay above the minimum legal speed of forty-five mph, and finally pushing the Harley up to seventy. At that point, I would have pushed a button to jettison the training wheels, like fuel tanks falling away from a space vehicle. Now that I'm booking it, I find that the Harley is behaving like a thoroughbred finally given its head, meant to run flat out, the only open question being: am I?

I am Jack Tanner, a fifty-two-year-old tax attorney with the largest law firm in Minneapolis. I am a devoted husband to my wife, Jenna; an adoring father to our daughter, Hope; a former Eagle Scout; a solid, civic-minded citizen who serves on committees and charitable boards; a good neighbor (at least I try to be); a recycler of refuse (although I have reasonable doubt about the value to the earth of doing this, having read in the *New York Times* that the amount of energy consumed in the recycling process outweighs the value of natural resources saved, but Jenna and Hope still want us to do it); a generous tipper if well-served, and sometimes even if not (a waitperson has to make a living); a payer of taxes (although I do take full advantage of loopholes in the tax codes); a voter who values character and qualifications over party affiliation; a registered organ donor; a contributor to charities Jenna and I consider worthy and to my undergraduate university and law school; a buyer of whatever a neighborhood kid comes to my door selling (especially if the product is Girl Scout cookies, Thin Mints being my weakness); a respectable fourteen handicap. If "salt of the earth" were not such a cliché, I might reasonably add that characteristic to my résumé, too.

I am, *prima facie*, the last kind of guy you'd expect to find—that I'd expect to find—leather-clad, booted, and bubble-helmeted, streaking toward the horizon astride a big-ass motorcycle at the beginning of a twenty-three hundred mile journey.

So far, it's going reasonably well, meaning that I haven't dumped the cycle, or chickened out and gone back home. Especially troublesome are the big semitrailer trucks, which create sucking vacuums as they pass that feel as if they could pull me under their wheels. Mercedes and BMW sedans have been my vehicles of choice, as soon as I could afford them, which is when I made partner at Hartfield, Miller, Simon & Swensen. Before then, it was Volvos and Saabs, chosen for their safety, quality, and affordability on an associate's salary, except for a red Pontiac GTO convertible with a 325-horse-power V8 and four-barrel carburetor, an indulgence Jenna kindly allowed me before our daughter was born.

As some men age, they feel the need to compensate for shrinking muscle mass and plummeting testosterone levels by wrapping themselves in valves and pistons and fuel-injected carburetion. They buy Porsche Turbos, or opt for the sport package on their family sedans, or drive big SUVs with all the off-road options: raised bodies, oversized tires, full-time four-wheel drive, and front brush guards, all ready for the Australian bush country, which they are unlikely to encounter on their way to work or to the dry cleaners. One of my friends has a tricked-out (magenta!) pickup truck; the only load I've ever seen in the rear bed is his golf clubs. A fortunate few ride the really big iron: private jets, or motor yachts the size of navy destroyers—a mine's-bigger-than-yours kind of thing.

But, for me, taking this long road trip on a fire-breathing, highway-eating, hard candy lucky green flake Harley-Davidson Road King Classic motorcycle isn't a male midlife crisis kind of thing. My crisis just happened to come at midlife and has nothing at all to do with shrinking muscle mass and declining testosterone levels.

2

I flip up my helmet's dark-tinted plastic face shield, wanting to feel the wind on my face, even if it means risking frostbite. Glancing skyward, I see a red-tailed hawk languidly riding the air currents rising off the rolling undulations of the Wisconsin farm fields on this perfect March morning. The rich black soil is still frozen; spring planting won't begin for at least another month when the farmers will sow the seeds for a nature's bounty of corn, soybeans, and alfalfa. Heartland America.

The hawk banks right, its gaze painting the landscape like a laser beam from a warplane's weapons system as it hunts breakfast: a rabbit, or mole, or snake. Absent that, road kill would do: flattened pancakes of fur, meat, blood, bone, and gristle, just like the carcass of some small animal I barely managed to avoid a few miles back.

Coming up on my right is a white two-story farmhouse behind a windbreak stand of jack pine. Near the house is the ramshackle skeleton of a red barn with a peeling, faded Mail Pouch Tobacco sign—"Chew Mail Pouch Tobacco/Treat Yourself To The Best"—painted on its side. Next to the barn is a newer outbuilding constructed of corrugated metal. Maybe a son has inherited this spread and, unlike most rural sons, has decided to remain on the land, declaring his commitment with the new structure. Or maybe that's a vision of farm life as outdated as the Mail Pouch sign, this spread now owned by an agribusiness corporation, its fields worked by tenant farmers, with an MBA overseer analyzing production quotas and commodity prices on his computer from an office in a city.

Powering up a long uphill grade, I come upon an eighteen-wheeler with a "How Am I Driving?" sign on the back, and an 800 number to call if anyone cares to answer the question or to apply for a driver's job. The big truck can only do fifty up the grade, so I gun the Harley—getting bolder now—and lean left into the passing lane.

The Road King's engine emits a rumbling, percussive, percolating sound: "potato-potato-potato" it seems to be saying, this exhaust note so distinctive, I once read in a law review article, that the Harley-Davidson Company of Milwaukee tried unsuccessfully to trademark it.

When I've run up beside the semi, I notice that it bears the name and logo of the Green Giant Company. It's a refrigerated truck, called a reefer, hauling frozen vegetables—peas, brussels sprouts, corn, green beans, lima beans—from the company's processing plant in Le Sueur, a small Minnesota town sixty miles south of Minneapolis. I know this because, over the years, I've posted hundreds of billable hours to my law firm's Green Giant account.

The trucker gives me a thumbs-up salute. I answer with a nod, still not confident enough to drive one-handed. This exchange pleases me. It is, at least in my mind, an initiation into the brotherhood of the open road. Or maybe he just likes the motorcycle.

A pale sun is just beginning to warm the land. I'm prepared for any weather. Along with the Harley, I purchased a complete riding ensemble: helmet, black leather jacket with zippered pockets, black leather chaps to wear over my jeans, black leather boots, and black leather gloves. A yellow rain suit is rolled into the saddlebags. Under my leathers, I'm wearing thermal underwear plus a flannel shirt and jeans; I'm comfortable enough, although sitting in my easy chair back home with a mug of hot coffee and the fireplace blazing would be better. Checking myself out in my full-length bedroom mirror this morning before heading out to the garage, I thought I looked more like the biker character in the Village People than an authentic Harley guy.

Four days ago, I bought my motorcycle at Hog Heaven, which is what the locals call the Harley-Davidson dealership on Broadway in Minneapolis. I call it Toyland.

"Hi there!" a woman called out as I entered the showroom. She walked over and offered her hand. "I'm Brenda and I'll be your server today." Like she was a waitress.

"Jack Tanner," I said.

"Feel free to look around, Jack, and let me know if you have any questions," she answered.

Brenda was pretty enough until she got close and I noticed the lines in her face, and that her shock of short blonde hair didn't likely come from her DNA. She was probably in her mid-to-late forties, and had a good body, an asset that could trump her flaws, in my opinion, especially if the bar was dark and you'd had a few beers. Well, she wasn't selling cosmetics in Neiman Marcus. Especially with the barbed wire tattoo around one of her biceps. Of course, this was a typical male, sexist analysis of the lady, and I'm no George Clooney myself, so who knows what she was thinking of the likes of me, walking into her dealership.

I told Brenda I was just browsing, which maybe I was, still undecided about my mode of transportation for my upcoming road trip. At that point, not knowing enough about the inventory to have any questions, I wandered around the big neon-illuminated showroom, admiring the rich, lustrous paint jobs and glistening chrome of the motorcycles. Just sitting there, leaning on their kickstands, they positively radiated kinetic energy. Just turn the key and I'm ready to rumble, they seemed to be thinking.

A full quarter of the floor space was devoted to Harley-Davidson merchandise, with racks and stacks of leathers and denims and sports clothes; helmets and boots and saddlebags;

and every manner of Harley logo items: coffee and beer mugs, baby clothes, metal-studded belts, dog collars and leashes (think pit bull), jewelry, coffee table books displaying sexy glamour shots of the bikes . . . Welcome to Harley World, I thought, it's not just a ride, it's a cult. Scientology on wheels. Did I really want to drink that Kool-Aid? Maybe it was too over-the-top for a guy like me—except for the overriding fact that I didn't want to be a guy like me anymore.

Brenda found me checking out a sleek black low-slung model displayed on a raised platform. I thought it looked like a panther, ready to hop down and run. A sign said it was a "V-Rod Night Rod Special," and could be mine for just shy of seventeen thousand bucks.

"So, Jack, any of these got your name on it?" Brenda asked. I hadn't realized she was standing behind me.

"Maybe."

Still not committed. Especially not to a custom job like the V-Rod. Maybe flying to Key West wasn't such a bad idea after all. Maybe staying home was an even better idea.

"Ever had a bike before?" Brenda wanted to know, although she must have known the answer. Had she ever had a customer wearing Topsiders?

"Not since my Schwinn."

I left out the part about the training wheels.

"Okay. We got Softails, Dyna Glides, Road Kings, Electra Glides, Sportsters, and these V-Rods. A ride for every occasion."

"I'm not sure what kind I want," I admitted.

"Not a problem," Brenda said. "How ya going to use it? Maybe take the wife to Dairy Queen on weekends?"

A logical conclusion.

"I'm planning a ride down to Florida."

Brenda looked impressed.

"Hey now. We got ourselves a player here." She began walking down the aisle. "Let's look over here."

She led me over to one of the rows where the biggest cycles were displayed.

"You'll want one of these heavy-duty touring models for a long haul, a Road King or Electra Glide. That way you'll arrive with your kidneys intact."

I walked over to one of the bikes. It was green, my favorite color, with sparkly flakes in the paint. The paint job seemed as good a way as any to choose, given that I was clueless about the actual machinery.

"That'd be my choice too," she said. "The Road King Classic, in hard candy lucky green flake. Sweet as they come. Big enough to eat up the interstates, but less bulky than the Electra Glides, which the cops favor." She patted the leather saddle. "Mount up, cowboy. Let's see how she fits."

It fit just fine.

I was startled a few minutes later, after I'd signed the sales contract and handed over my credit card, earning lots of airline miles, when a man behind the parts counter began ringing a brass ship's bell bolted on the wall: BONG! BONG! BONG!

When the ringing stopped, all available dealership staff shouted out, "Another Harley owner! Welcome to the family!" This reminded me of those T.G.I. Friday's kind of restaurants where the wait staff surrounds your table to sing "Happy Birthday." Surveying the showroom crew and the other customers who were roaming around, none of whom looked like a tax attorney, I felt that it was maybe like joining the Manson family.

I arranged with Brenda to have my motorcycle delivered, after the service department had prepped it. "You'll need some leathers and a helmet," she said as she led me to the apparel section. Before we were done, all of those items, plus a pair of boots and riding gloves, were piled on the checkout counter, bar code tags being scanned by a young woman wearing an Aerosmith tee shirt revealing a pierced navel and jeans so tight they looked as if they'd been spray-painted on.

"You can get a cycle license learner's permit at any DMV office," Brenda told me when my gear was bagged up. "Then you practice driving until you're ready for your road test, which consists of driving around cones in the DMV office parking lot, piece of cake, and they'll add an endorsement on your driver's license."

I hadn't thought about that, and had no time for the road test, because if I delayed my planned departure, I might not depart. I'd have to make it to Florida on the learner's permit. When—if—I made it there, I'd certainly be ready for the DMV's parking lot cones.

On the way home from the dealership, I wondered if I should name my new motorcycle. It would be my companion on the long journey. Maybe Pegasus, the winged steed of Greek mythology. Or Rocinante, the name of Don Quixote's horse. In the end, I decided not to name it. Too cutesy, too precious, like those stupid boat names I've always hated: *Dad's Dream, E-Z-Livin', She Got The House, Babes on Waves*, all of which I'd seen on Minnesota lakes.

The next morning, I went to the DMV to get a booklet describing the requirements for a motorcycle endorsement on my driver's license, and that afternoon, I passed the test for the learner's permit. For this, I had to learn such rules as: passengers may not ride on a motorcycle unless they can reach the footrests on each side of the motorcycle with both feet while seated. No bar exam, but I did have to read the booklet.

CRUISING ALONG the interstate, feeling free as that hawk I saw, I remember the time I arrived home after work and found Jenna in the kitchen, washing lettuce in the sink. Her shoulder-length strawberry blonde hair swirled sexily as she turned to greet me. She was wearing a white cotton turtleneck and black jeans. The turtleneck stretched over her breasts, her nipples visible through the thin fabric. No bra. She had something more than dinner in mind.

She crossed to the pantry on some invented errand so I could see her fine little bottom move under the denim like a sack full of cats on the way to the river. Jenna the tease. I walked up behind her, and kissed her neck. She said, "Hey sailor, whatta ya got in mind?" And then it was shore leave time, right there on the granite center island.

The summer before my third year of law school at the University of Michigan in Ann Arbor, where I also did my undergraduate work, I decided to backpack around Europe with Peter Linden, another law student. We wanted to see something of the world before beginning the grind of being junior associates at a law firm.

Peter and I bought Eurail passes and traveled from Luxembourg, which is where the budget-priced turboprop planes of Icelandic Air landed, to Switzerland, Germany, and the Netherlands. We had a good time drinking beer, eating the local cuisines that we could afford on our meager budget, and seeing the sights. I had my Nikon, and Peter, who worked as a folksinger to earn spending money in school, had his Martin steel-string guitar.

One morning, over espresso and muffins in Amsterdam, I told Peter, "We've got three weeks left before beginning our indentured servitude back in the States, and there is one thing this tour is lacking."

"What's that?" he asked.

"Women."

We'd attempted to strike up conversations with a number of local females, even joined some for lunches and museum tours, very nice girls, but in the end, the language barrier prevented the relationships from progressing. At least in my view. Or maybe it was that we didn't launder our clothes very often, which we didn't.

"No problem," Peter said. "I have the answer."

"And that is?"

"Paris, city of light, city of love."

"But we don't speak French," I said. "Sure, lots of French girls speak English, but that narrows the field."

"Trust me," he responded.

The following day, we disembarked at the Gare du Nord station in Paris, checked our guidebook, and walked to the Left Bank, where cheap rooms were to be had. The first small hotels and rooming houses we tried were full. We found a little pension on the Île de la Cité that had a room, a sixth-floor walk-up. We discovered, at the stroke of the hour, and every hour thereafter, why the room was available. It was right near the bell tower of Notre-Dame Cathedral.

"Okay, time to implement the plan," Peter said when the ringing stopped.

I followed him down the stairs and across the Pont-Neuf, which, the guidebook told us, was the oldest standing bridge across the Seine, connecting the island to the Left Bank. On the mainland side, Peter took his guitar out of the case and began singing American folk songs, the point being, I imagined, that the songs might attract women who could speak at least some English. Perhaps faulty logic, but the only plan we had.

For the first hour, some passersby tossed franc notes into the open guitar case, and moved on, or ignored us entirely. Then, as Peter was into the Kingston Trio song "Tom Dooley," two very attractive young ladies stopped. One of them asked, "Are you Americans?" By her accent, I knew she was, too.

That's how we met Laurie and Anne, who were on a European tour following their graduation from a Catholic women's college in Milwaukee. We shut down the concert, had lunch together at a Left Bank café, walked and talked, and toured the Louvre.

"So how about dinner tonight?" Peter asked them, happy to have found girls who could actually understand the invitation.

"Not tonight," Laurie said. "We have other plans."

I must have looked disappointed, which I was, but Anne added, "We're traveling with another friend. She's not feeling well, stomach problem, so we're eating at our hotel tonight. Why don't you meet us for lunch tomorrow at Café de Flore.

Do you know it? It's on Boulevard Saint-Germaine. You could meet us there, and if our friend is feeling better, she'll join us."

And that's how I met Jenna Lockhart of Birmingham, Michigan.

Until then, I'd always thought that the concept of love at first sight was a myth. Now I don't.

Jenna. My poor, wounded wife.

I wonder if I should remind her of moments like that time in the kitchen when I stop to see her at The Sanctuary, the private psychiatric hospital in McLean, Virginia, where she has been living for nearly nine months. Would she want to remember them? I'm never certain, on my way to these visits, whether she wants to remember anything at all about our past life. Maybe that would only add to her pain.

It was my duty as a husband and father to protect both of the women in my life. Jenna and Hope. But I found out that I could protect neither one of them, or myself, from the sudden, random evil in this world.

3

I hear a loud whoop-whoop-whoop sound behind me. In the rearview mirror I see the flashing lights of a Wisconsin State Patrol cruiser, coming up fast. I check the speedometer. Daydreaming and doing seventy-six.

I slow down and pull onto the gravel shoulder, kicking up stones, and stop. I push down the kickstand with my left boot and ease the weight of the big cycle onto it. It's a heavy mother. If it tips over, I don't know if I could pick it up without the trooper's help, which would be embarrassing.

I turn in the saddle and see that the trooper has parked behind me. After a moment, the trooper gets out, slips on his Smokey Bear hat—they love to get all duded up in those hats and boots and jodhpurs, like Canadian Mounties—and takes a few steps toward me, then stops. I stoically await my fate: a speeding ticket, my first in years. Now my insurance rate will go up.

He calls out in a loud, clipped, no-nonsense voice, right on the edge of courtesy, but clearly not to be disregarded: "Please sir, step off the motorcycle."

I hesitate, wondering if they are always this cautious in Wisconsin on a routine traffic stop. Then I remember I don't look like my usual, respectable, solid-citizen self. I'm a motorcycle guy in leathers, with the helmet bubble hiding my face. Potentially dangerous. Maybe fitting the description of another cycle rider who just robbed a bank or escaped from prison.

I don't want my journey to end here on the gravel shoulder of I-94 somewhere in Wisconsin with a bullet hole in my new leather jacket, which cost four hundred forty dollars. Or spread-eagled on the ground with my face in the gravel, arms cuffed behind my back. So I dismount, and stand facing the trooper. Even though I haven't been told to, I keep my hands in sight, which, I know from cop shows, they want you to do.

"Thank you, sir," the trooper says, and walks toward me. I notice that his right hand is resting on his pistol. "Take off your helmet, then lean forward against the seat with your feet spread wide."

Again, I hesitate. This entire situation is so utterly unfamiliar. The trooper says, more sternly, with no "sir" attached this time, "Do. It. Now."

I comply, resting my hands on the saddle, my legs a yard apart, the limit of my range of motion these days. Just like in the movies. The difference being that in the movies the trooper's gun is loaded with blanks. He comes up behind me and pats me down. This is all very surreal.

"That's fine, sir," he says when he's finished, a degree of professional cop courtesy returning to his voice. "Now stand up, please."

"I'm a lawyer," I blurt out as I stand and turn to face him. I instantly regret saying such a stupid thing. To a law enforcement officer, it's probably better to be an outlaw biker than one of those scum-sucking, bottom-feeding attorneys who subvert justice with their courtroom tricks.

"I'll need to see your driver's license please," the trooper says. His gold nameplate reads, "Cpl. Jensen."

"Sure, officer, no problem," I answer, as cooperatively and unthreateningly as I can.

"Trooper, not officer," he corrects me.

A slip. I know he's a state trooper but I'm under some pressure here. Trooper must be higher on the law-enforcement hierarchy. Cpl. Jensen looks to me like a teenager, barely old enough to drive, let alone enforce the traffic laws, the same way the Minnesota Twins starting lineup and summer interns at the law firm now appear to a man my age. One of the milestones in the aging process.

My helmet slides off the saddle, where I balanced it, and onto the ground: one hundred eight dollars worth of shiny black polycarbonate shell with anti-fog face shield and removable, washable, antibacterial lining, now dinged up by gravel. I unbuckle one side of my black leather saddlebags and fish out my wallet. I notice that as my hand went into the saddlebags, Cpl. Jensen's hand returned to his pistol. I also know from cop shows that I should take the license out and not hand over the wallet, lest it appear a bribe is being offered. I do this now.

He takes my Minnesota driver's license, looks at it and says, "There's no motorcycle endorsement."

I take the folded paper learner's permit out of the wallet and hand it to him. He looks at it, then says, "Please remain here for a moment, sir."

He returns to the cruiser, gets in, running my name on his onboard computer, I'm certain, looking for any outstanding warrants. Then he gets out, walks back to me, and begins the usual dialogue of the routine traffic stop, the kind that does not involve a shoot-out, which is a relief. I'm a speeder, not a felon.

"Do you know what the speed limit is here, Mr. Tanner?"

"I'm sorry, I didn't notice any signs."

I know that ignorance of the law is no excuse, but why not give it a shot.

"It's seventy," he informs me. "Do you know how fast you were traveling?"

"No," I fib.

I know that lying to a law enforcement officer is a felony, but how can he prove that I know the speed limit, or how fast I was going? My lawyer's mind at work, inappropriately for what is now a routine situation.

"I clocked you at just under eighty at the top of that rise back there," he says.

"I guess I wasn't paying attention," I say truthfully. I know better than to speed on highways in Wisconsin, where traffic fines are notoriously a big revenue source for the state. But I guess that I've been on an adrenaline high ever since starting this trip. I need to dial it down a notch and keep my head in the game.

Instead of writing a citation, Cpl. Jensen touches the saddle of my motorcycle, as if petting a horse.

"A Road King," he says. "Nice bike. Had it long?"

"Not very long."

"Okay, Mr. Tanner, this is a warning. Slow down. I've had to clean up after more than a few accidents involving motorcycles coming up against cars and trucks, and the cycle *always* loses."

Road kill.

He nods and strides back to his cruiser, opens the door, then turns back and says, "Slow down and drive safely. By the way, Mr. Tanner, where are you headed?"

"I'm just out for a joy ride," I tell him.

Which could not be further from the truth.

DOWN THE highway another twenty minutes, a sign announces the Eau Claire exit, with the promise of Food/Gas/Lodging. I swing onto the exit ramp feeding onto a two-lane road lined with gas stations, fast food restaurants and chain motels: the kind of ubiquitous neon strip that has replaced small town Main Streets. No sense of place anymore when everywhere looks alike. However, this particular stretch of road holds a special memory for me.

One long-ago Christmas Eve morning, when our world was newer and anything seemed possible, even lifelong joy, Jenna, Hope, and I stayed at the Holiday Inn I'm rolling past. We were heading for Milwaukee, to spend the holiday with Jenna's parents, and her two sisters and their families.

I thought we shouldn't risk the drive because an early morning snowstorm was building in intensity; it was very cold and the highway was getting slippery, even with snow tires. We made it as far as Eau Claire after creeping along over black ice, past cars that had slid into ditches and fields. When a state trooper directed us around a second jackknifed semi, Jenna said that we should stop and wait out the storm.

It was clearly not going to let up anytime soon, so I got a room for us at the Holiday Inn because it advertised a swimming pool under a geodesic dome, which I knew Hope would love.

The storm raged all night. Christmas Eve dinner was cheeseburgers, milkshakes, and fries in our room from a McDonald's beside the hotel, which I walked to. I got a plain burger for our dog Cookie, a Bichon, the desk clerk having waived the hotel's no-pet rule for us orphans of the storm.

We watched an Andy Williams Christmas special on TV and were as cozy and happy as we'd ever been on a Christmas Eve. By morning, the weather was clear, the landscape covered with a white frosting right out of a Currier and Ives holiday print. We arrived in Milwaukee late Christmas morning. Hope mentioned that trip every Christmas Eve for years: remember when we drove to grandpa and grandma's in the snowstorm and stayed at the hotel with the pool and had hamburgers? Can we do that again this year?

Now I'm certain I shouldn't mention these kinds of memories to Jenna, because they are so very painful for me. For her, in the condition she's in, they would be torture.

CRUISING THE Eau Claire strip, I notice a large number of trucks and cars parked at a Happy Chef Restaurant. I didn't have breakfast other than coffee and OJ this morning. I'm hungry. According to the mythology of the open road, the presence of the trucks is a good sign, so I pull into the parking lot. I hadn't yet discovered, but would before my ride was done, that the truck count outside a highway restaurant says more about the adequacy of the parking lot, and availability of showers for the drivers, than about the quality of the food.

Roger Miller's "King of the Road" is playing on the sound system as I enter the restaurant, the perfect theme song for this time and place. King of the Road on a Road King. That's me. But I won't say that out loud, not in here, where the real road kings dine.

I find a stool at the counter and scan the menu, not noticing until I'm seated that I'm in a section of the dining room, which, according to a sign on a stand, is reserved for "professional drivers." But I go unchallenged and decide to stay where I am. I am a professional, and I am a driver, just not the kind they mean.

A waitress behind the counter comes over, fills my coffee cup, and asks, "What's your pleasure, sweetie?" She looks as if she's logged a lot of miles behind diner counters. Her name-tag says she's Sally.

I order the Open Roader: eggs, pancakes, bacon, and hash browns, which is the kind of breakfast I'd imagined being served in that farmhouse fifty miles back, and the kind of food I've avoided, for health reasons, ever since I turned fifty, my usual breakfast being oatmeal with banana and wheat germ. But clogged arteries are the least of my concerns at the moment, and I am, after all, sitting among professional drivers. Go big or go home is my new motto.

A man seated on the stool beside mine says, without looking up from his food, "So, you're on a cycle." It's my leathers. "What kind?"

His denim jacket has Peterbilt and American flag patches. He looks to be in his late fifties or early sixties, wiry like a rodeo cowboy. He's having pork chops and mashed potatoes for breakfast.

"I'm Ray," he says, looking over at me now. "Ray Price." No handshake, his hands are occupied with utensils.

"A Harley," I answer, proud I can tell this guy wearing the flag I'd bought American. I swivel on my stool and offer my hand. "Jack Tanner." He puts down his fork and returns the handshake.

"Had an Electra Glide once," he tells me. "Which I dumped on the way home from Sturgis when some jackass in a car heading the other way swerved to avoid a deer and ran me into a ditch. Now I have a stainless steel plate in my hip and I stick to the eighteen-wheelers."

Not something I particularly wanted to hear. He takes a swallow of coffee and asks, "So, where're you heading?"

I'm tempted to blurt out the truth, but instead I tell him, "Oh, you know. Typical midlife crisis (a lie.) Buy a motorcycle, take it out on the highway to see what it'll do, and get some breakfast."

The joyride dodge again. I ask Ray where he's going.

"Driving from Bismarck to Chicago with a load of hogs. Some of 'em may end up on the menu here," he says. He downs the last of his coffee, stands and says, "Had my own midlife crisis some years ago. My buddy Jack Daniels helped me through it, though I don't recommend that route. Safe trip, Jack."

He picks up his check, drops a five-dollar bill onto the counter, and heads for the cash register stand near the door. I finish my breakfast, leave a five-dollar tip for Sally, too, and head for the parking lot. The song playing as I leave is "Born To Be Wild."

4

Traffic is heavier now, especially the big trucks in a hurry to get from here to there to deliver their loads on schedule. It always annoyed me, in a car, when they would run right up on my tailpipe when I was in the right-hand lane, and then, if the right lane was still obstructed, they would pop out behind me when I swung out into the passing lane, pushing me to speed. But on the cycle, I discover that I can bob and weave through traffic, more confident now, maybe foolishly so. As I do, I notice disapproving looks from some drivers, as if I'm a badass, nonconformist outlaw. Good. Lock the doors and hide the women and children, here comes an outlaw (who could help you with your tax return).

A gap in the traffic. I power up a rise, the highway bordered on the left by the limestone cliffs of the Wisconsin Dells, and open farmland on the right. I check my watch. About half an hour to Madison, home of the University of Wisconsin, my first destination.

I LEAN the cycle onto the Madison exit and turn left onto Johnson Street, which runs between Lake Monona on the left and Lake Mendota on the right, enjoying the scenic view, unobstructed by the confines of a car.

Madison is a little gem of a college town, always ranking highly on those best-places-to-live lists. But for the past year Madison has, for me, taken on the stark grimness of a crime scene. Which, for the Tanner family, it is.

I veer right onto University Avenue and turn through the main gate of the University of Wisconsin campus. Students turn at the sound of the Harley. The engine noise also attracts the attention of a university security guard on a motor scooter, the kind with an enclosed cab and small truck bed on the back. I notice that the guard is wearing a black snowmobile suit. My Harley could eat that little putt-putt for lunch and still have room for dessert. A few hours on a Harley-Davidson and I've become an arrogant son of a bitch.

Campus security, what a joke. I feel the urge to drive around shouting a warning to every coed I encounter: *Be careful! Don't go out alone!* Of course, this would be madness. These girls would just stare at the lunatic on a motorcycle, maybe call 911 on their cell phones. I'd be the one who would frighten them. The Devil among them.

A couple is strolling on the sidewalk with their backs toward me: a girl with shoulder-length blonde hair, wearing jeans and a green ski parka, and a tall boy in khaki slacks and a varsity letter jacket. This is a Division I school. Big-time athletics. The boy must be good at whatever sport he plays. In case of trouble, I hope he's around to protect her.

From the back, the girl looks like my daughter, Hope. All of these college girls look like Hope to me: young, beautiful, happily oblivious to the true nature of the world, on their way to class, or their dorm rooms or apartments, or Starbucks. . . . On their way to their futures, careers if they want, husbands, first houses, children. They can have it all, they are certain. Let them think that, as long as they can. I will not tell them otherwise. I will not share the awful knowledge I've sadly acquired about what can happen when God looks the other way.

North along Campus Drive, then right onto Highland Avenue, which runs along the western boundary of the campus. I turn onto Hiawatha Street, with its rows of student rental apartment buildings: converted Victorian houses, cinder block and brick mid-rise buildings, ranch house style duplexes. Oak and maples line the street, their spring buds coming out.

I pull up and park in front of 310 Hiawatha, a four-story tan brick 1950s apartment building. Sitting astride the Harley, I watch young men and women, some wearing backpacks, some plugged into iPods or chatting on cell phones, pass in and out of the building.

On a late August Saturday afternoon, about a year and a half ago, I arrived here driving a U-Haul truck, with Jenna and Hope, the truck loaded with furniture and Hope's clothing. She was excited to be moving into an apartment off-campus after a year in the freshman dorm. On the night of March 1 during that sophomore year, Hope got a cell phone call, then left the apartment she shared with two other girls, telling them she would be back in an hour or so. She didn't say who called her or where she was going. It was about ten P.M., one of her roommates told police. No, it was more like eleven, the other said. Hope was wearing jeans and a red sweater, one said. No, it was a grey University of Wisconsin sweatshirt and black tights, the other said.

Such is the reliability of eyewitnesses, I was told by Detective Lieutenant Vernon Douglas of the Madison Police Department, when Jenna and I arrived in Madison two days later. Vernon Douglas is a tall, muscular, middle-aged black man who looks like he could have played football for a Division I school, which, I later learned, he did, at Michigan State. When two or more people invent a story, he explained, that story is identical. But honest recollections by witnesses almost never match.

Everyone involved with the victim of a crime goes onto the list of suspects, Detective Douglas told us, even two sweet girls like Hope's roommates, Maureen Fox from Fargo, North Dakota, and Sherry Silverman from Plainfield, New Jersey, who were quickly eliminated. Jenna and I met them and their parents the day Hope moved into the apartment. We all went to dinner that night. Everyone was very nice.

Hope was supposed to meet Maureen the following day at the Counseling and Guidance Services Office to get details about the university's Junior Year Abroad program. They'd talked about applying to study at the University of Florence or the Sorbonne in Paris. When Hope didn't show up for the meeting, Maureen tried to call her on her cell phone. Hope didn't answer, and she didn't come back to the apartment that night. The next morning, Maureen and Sherry went to the Campus Police Department. The campus police spent an hour checking, and found that Hope had not attended any of her classes the previous day. That's when the campus police chief called the Madison Police Department.

Hope frequently spent the night at her boyfriend Slater Babcock's apartment, her roommates told Detective Douglas. Hope had never mentioned Slater's name to Jenna or me, just saying that she was currently dating "a nice guy who plays lacrosse." When she left the apartment that night, she took her cell phone and keys, but not her wallet or any overnight gear. Her yellow VW Beetle convertible was still parked on the street.

Jenna answered the call from the dean of students. In a panic, she called me at my office and told me our daughter was missing. Two hours later, we were on a flight to Madison.

I rented a car at the Dane County Regional Airport and we drove directly to the Madison Police Department headquarters for a briefing by Detective Douglas. I didn't know him well enough then to call him Vernon, but, before long, I would.

Earlier that afternoon, he'd brought Slater Babcock from his classroom to headquarters. Slater called his father, and then told Detective Douglas that he wanted an attorney. Slater's father, Charles Babcock, an investment banker from Stamford, Connecticut, hired a Milwaukee criminal defense attorney to represent his son, once the police identified him as a "person of interest."

Hope and Slater had been dating for about two months, Maureen and Sherry had told Douglas. He was a "spoiled rich kid from Connecticut," they said, but, as far as they knew, he had never threatened or harmed Hope or anyone else. He didn't seem like that kind of person, they said. They didn't think Hope was very serious about Slater, she just enjoyed his company.

Before we arrived, Slater was allowed to leave the police department headquarters, where he'd spent two hours in an interrogation room, refusing to answer questions until his attorney was present. The next day, with both his attorney and his father present, he came back and was questioned by Detective Douglas. Over the next three days, he was also questioned by a state police detective, and an FBI agent from Milwaukee.

Slater Babcock never wavered from his story. Yes, he'd spoken with Hope by cell phone on the night she disappeared, but they hadn't talked about her coming to his apartment, which was a half-mile away from Hope's. Whenever they spent the night together it was at his place because he lived alone. Sometimes she came over unannounced to surprise him. Maybe that's what she was doing. She often walked instead of driving because his building had no parking lot, finding a spot on the street at night was difficult, and Hope liked the exercise.

Interviews with Slater's neighbors produced no evidence that Hope was at his apartment that night, but there was no reason for them to know about that anyway, unless they happened to see her outside. There being no evidence of Slater's involvement in Hope's disappearance, he was told there would be no further questions at this time, but to notify Douglas if he was planning to leave the area.

I told Detective Douglas that I wanted to speak with Slater, but he ordered me not to talk to him, or get anywhere near him, because I might say or do something that could be prejudicial to the case and also get me into a great deal of trouble.

During our first meeting with Detective Douglas, he assured Jenna and me that the department was "bringing its full resources to bear upon the case."

I was shocked when he said "the case." Our daughter was now a "case," a police file number. I couldn't tell if Jenna picked up on that, and I didn't mention it to her later.

Detective Douglas asked us if Hope had any history of "going off on her own" without telling us. It happened, he said. It was a possibility he had to explore. Last year, a female student went to Cancun with friends during spring break after telling her parents she had to stay on campus to study for exams. The parents found out when they decided to drive to Madison from their home in Green Bay to surprise their daughter with a care package of her favorite goodies, and take her to dinner. Douglas tracked her down.

I was distressed to learn, from his business card, that Vernon Douglas was a homicide detective, and I told him this. Homicide, as in murder. So the police were assuming that Hope was dead rather than just missing?

"We have two other detectives in the department," he responded. "One specializes in thefts and robberies, the other provides general backup wherever needed. It was the chief's call. I've been around the longest, and finding your daughter is the department's top priority. Believe me, we're doing everything that can be done. We've called in the FBI, we're monitoring her credit cards and cell phone activity. We've looked at her Facebook page, e-mails, blogs and Tweets. So far, nothing from those avenues. But we're not stopping."

On the morning of our second day in Madison, Jenna and I met with Winton Toller, the university's dean of students. Toller informed us that a convicted sex offender who lived near the campus had been cleared by police; he was in the hospital for an appendectomy the day Hope disappeared.

I asked the dean how in the hell a sex offender could be allowed to live in a neighborhood near the campus. Were there other felons in the neighborhood? Murderers out on parole? Armed robbers wearing ankle bracelets? Dean Toller, an affable and portly man in his sixties who wore tweeds and a bow tie, was a professor of economics who had held the dean's job for the past six years.

Toller said that his office had been notified by the police department about the man a year ago, but the law allowed him to live where he wanted, as long as he registered with the police, which he had. The dean hadn't been notified that any other such people currently lived near the university, he said.

Why weren't parents of students told about the sex offender, I asked him. I'm an attorney, I said, and will look into the possibility that the university had some degree of liability for what's happened. Dean Toller responded by saying that no one yet knows if any crime has occurred, and we're all hoping for the best, but the university will certainly review its policies on such matters.

"Maybe you should try harder to keep track of your students instead of reviewing your policies," I said as Jenna and I left his office.

On our fourth day in Madison, I insisted that Jenna return home, convincing her that she should be there in case Hope called or showed up, although I didn't think either of these possibilities likely. By that time, Jenna was mainly staying in our room at the Madison Concourse Hotel anyway, and was becoming increasingly frantic. Before she boarded an American Eagle turboprop at Dane County Regional Airport, she said to me, "She's gone, Jack. I know we'll never see our daughter again and our life will never be the same."

I told her that it was too soon to give up. Didn't that kidnapped girl in Utah, whose name I couldn't remember, turn up eighteen months later? "We'll never give up looking for Hope," I said, giving my wife a hug and a kiss when her flight was called.

When I said that, I meant that we would never give up trying to find our daughter alive. But now I realize that there is very little chance of that. Now, the best I can do is to try to find out what happened to her, and maybe bring her body home.

I remained in Madison another three days, checking in with Douglas daily, and driving the campus and city streets in my rental car. I put up missing-person fliers with Hope's name and photo on them, which I had made at a local copy shop, wherever I could find a spot around campus and in surrounding neighborhoods, alongside the fliers for missing dogs and cats.

Lyle Ferguson, the Hartfield, Miller managing partner, called to say that I should take all the time I needed, but I knew that my partners would at some point lose patience with my sabbatical from billable hours, even given the circumstances.

W<small>HEN</small> I arrived back home, I greeted Jenna in the kitchen. She cheerfully welcomed me back as if I'd been on a business trip and said, "I think I'll have a cup of tea. Would you like one too?"

"You know I never drink tea," I said.

"Oh, I guess I forgot."

She put the teapot on the gas range and went into the laundry room as I carried my suitcase upstairs. I was unpacking when I heard the teapot whistling, and keep on whistling. I went down to the kitchen, poured a cup of tea for her, and found Jenna sitting in the family room.

"I fixed your tea," I told her.

"Thank you," she said, "but I don't think I'll have any."

I went back upstairs to finish unpacking, pausing outside Hope's bedroom. The door was closed. Hope always kept it open, even when she was sleeping, and we'd kept it that way since she left for college. This habit began when she was very young and imagined that some fearsome creature was lurking under her bed, or in her closet, or on a ladder just outside her window, ready to snatch her when the lights went off. When she cried out, one of us would pad down the hallway and sit with her until she fell asleep, or take her into our bed, assuring her that she was safe, and believing it then. Now Jenna had closed the door.

I opened the door and went in, saddened again by the usual accoutrements of a happy, well-adjusted young woman's life: the frilly canopied bed covered with pillows and stuffed animals; her field hockey and lacrosse sticks; the cork board mounted on one wall, displaying concert ticket stubs, withered wrist corsages; photos of Hope with friends mugging for the camera; Edina High School and University of Wisconsin banners; and all the other artifacts of the living Hope.

Already, I thought, after less than two weeks since she'd gone missing, our daughter's bedroom was taking on the look of one of those period rooms preserved in a museum where no one has ever lived. Maybe I should string a velvet rope across the doorway.

I moved to Hope's bed, turned back the spread, and touched her pillow, irrationally hoping to find it warm. I walked over to the window and looked out at the oak tree in the backyard. Hope's bedroom is not the largest of the four in the house. Other than the master, one of the other rooms has quite a bit more square footage, and a bigger closet. Jenna chose this room as Hope's nursery because it's closest to our bedroom. When Hope was twelve, we asked her if she wanted to move into the larger bedroom, but she said no, she loved the view of the backyard with that big oak tree that was home to a squirrel family. She named the squirrels, pretending that she could distinguish one from another.

I replaced the spread and went out of the bedroom, leaving the door open. I wondered what could possibly come next for Jenna and me, other than to keep on waiting for Hope to reappear in some form or other, so we could either celebrate the miracle of her safe return, or hold a memorial service and try to get on with our lives, whatever that meant.

Please, let all this be a dream and let me wake up now, I thought. This would be a good time to start believing in God so that my prayer would at least be considered. If there were a God, then there would be someone to petition when bad things happened to good people. A cosmic appellate court. But to me, any view of history would suggest that such appeals merely rise up into the black void of the universe, either unheard or ignored, certiorari neither granted nor denied. Of what relevance is a Prime Mover who does not intervene in human affairs? Of what use is a Supreme Being who allows wars and pandemics and tsunamis and the death of innocents? Did Jews lose their faith as the Zyklon B gas came hissing out of the showerheads at Auschwitz-Birkenau and Treblinka? If religion truly is the opiate of the masses, well, maybe I could will myself to believe just enough to ease my pain and to maintain some level of functionality. But I could not make myself believe.

A month later, I suggested that Jenna start seeing a psychiatrist. He gave her a prescription for depression, and this seemed to help her somewhat, but she was clearly not herself. I suppose I wasn't myself either. Two lost souls, wandering around in a house that now seemed too big for us, and too empty. The medication didn't seem to help Jenna that much, and two months later her psychiatrist suggested that she should consider inpatient treatment. He recommended The Sanctuary in McLean, Virginia.

We lost our beloved daughter on March 1 one year ago. Today, on this sad anniversary of that life-changing event, I've chosen to start my journey.

5

The story of the disappearance of a female University of Wisconsin student was big news locally and nationally. During the weeks after it happened, Jenna and I appeared on cable and network TV news shows and radio programs, and did interviews with newspapers and some magazines, appealing for help in locating our daughter. All of this was arranged by a Minneapolis public relations firm on retainer to my law firm. This was uncomfortable for us, we were private people, but we'd have done anything that might bring our daughter home.

Jenna was particularly touched when, during one interview, a pretty, blonde female network news reporter teared up, causing her to tear up too, the camera close on their faces, I saw in a replay later that night. I cynically told Jenna I thought this was staged, then regretted saying it. I believe it was, but why not let Jenna believe that the reporter felt our pain?

I remembered the photos of missing children that had appeared on the sides of milk cartons—"Have you seen this child?"—and briefly considered legal action to force the Wisconsin Dairy Products Association to bring back the campaign. Lyle Ferguson reminded me that one of the larger dairies in the state was an important client of the firm, so I dropped the idea.

At first, I returned to Madison every few weeks. After that, it was every few months, and then less often. I would always drive around the campus as if Hope might suddenly appear coming out of the student center or driving by in the yellow Beetle, her high school graduation present. During each trip to Madison, I would visit with Vernon Douglas, who seemed genuinely frustrated at having no progress to report.

Finally, I stopped coming to Madison, until today. The Madison Police Department, the Wisconsin State Police, and the FBI have had long enough to find out what happened to my daughter. Now it is time for her father to try.

I've LOST track of the time. How long have I been sitting here on the Harley, staring at this apartment building? My wristwatch tells me it's been nearly half an hour. As I shut down the engine, I'm startled to see Maureen Fox, one of Hope's former roommates, come out of the apartment building. She must still live here. She'd be a junior now. Short dark hair, tall . . . But she's wearing sunglasses, so I'm not certain.

She heads down the front walk toward me, then abruptly turns and goes back into the building. Did she recognize me? I couldn't blame her for not wanting to relive such a bad memory by speaking with Hope's father. But no, she couldn't have recognized me, not dressed in leathers, sitting on a motorcycle. If I were wearing a golf shirt and khakis, and driving a car, maybe. Maureen, or whoever that was, must have just forgotten something.

After a while, I hear a car and turn in the saddle to see a Madison Police Department cruiser parking behind me. A female officer gets out and walks over. She wears sergeant's stripes. Her nameplate says "Sgt. Bradford." She looks to be in her midthirties, pretty, with short dark hair, and a trim body under her tailored uniform. Maybe a psych major who couldn't find other employment in this recession, or a single mother working her way through law school. Or maybe just someone who likes police work.

"Hello, sir," she says as I slide off the seat and open one of the flaps on the saddlebags, reflexively intending to get my driver's license and registration.

She takes a step backward, letting her right hand casually drop to the snap on the strap that secures her pistol in its holster.

"I need you to step away from the cycle, sir, and show me your hands," she says.

Oh, that's right, I'm an outlaw of the open road. I obey, thinking, here we go again.

"Hello officer," I say. "Is there a problem?"

"We had a call about a man on a motorcycle watching people going in and out of this apartment building. These are student apartments, so we like to keep track of who's hanging around the neighborhood."

"Yes, of course," I tell her. "My daughter lived here when she was a student. Just thought I'd stop by and take a look."

Without taking her hand off the pistol, she says, "Okay, sir. But I need to see your driver's license and registration."

I find my wallet in the saddlebags, extract my license, motorcycle learner's permit, and cycle registration, and offer them to the sergeant, letting her come to me. She takes them and returns to the cruiser. After a few minutes, she gives me back my paperwork, which I put back into my wallet.

"Okay, Mr. Tanner. Do you have business in Madison, other than visiting your daughter's apartment building?"

"I'm a friend of Detective Vernon Douglas," I tell her. "We're getting together today."

"Detective Douglas? I guess it's been awhile since you've seen him."

"A while, I guess," I tell her.

"He's Chief Douglas now, ever since Chief Margulies retired." She nods toward the Harley. "Road King. Had it long?"

"One week."

"A week. And driving all the way from Minneapolis on a learner's permit. Well don't let that bad boy get away from you." Walking back to the cruiser, she adds, "So long, Mr. Tanner. You be safe now."

So far, everyone who finds me driving a motorcycle tells me to be safe. I swing up onto the saddle and start the engine, thinking: I left "safe" behind when I walked into that Harley dealership.

6

I check into the Madison Concourse Hotel on West Dayton Street, where I always stay when in town. I park the Harley in the hotel garage myself, realizing that I've become protective of my bike and worried about how the valet would handle it.

My room has a view of the big domed white-granite state capitol building, which is quite imposing when illuminated at night. I toss the saddlebags onto a chair—the Harley has built-in plastic saddlebags compartments but I also bought a leather one to use as luggage—undress, and take a long, steamy shower, washing away the road grit and easing my aching muscles.

The shower finished, I find the TV remote and flop onto the bed. MSNBC is headlining a story about the conviction of a thirty-two-year-old female high school English teacher on charges of child molestation and statutory rape for having sex with a fifteen-year-old male student. There is video of the teacher walking into the courthouse with her attorney, wearing a form-fitting black knit dress and black spike heels. She is an absolute knockout: tall and thin, beautiful, long blonde hair, blue eyes. I think what every man must think when seeing this story: Hey lady, you could do better than some pimply high school kid. And also: Where were teachers like that when I was in high school? I know better than to express either of those thoughts to a woman.

The teacher reminds me of Susan Toth, if you add twenty years. Susan and Henry Toth are neighbors and members of a bridge group Jenna and I belong to. Susan called me a week after I took Jenna to The Sanctuary. Jenna had gone willingly, like a nun entering a convent to be sheltered from the world, it seemed to me.

I was surprised that Susan knew about this. Jenna had not mentioned it to anyone, as far as I knew. Our vague plan was to say that Susan was traveling to Europe with an old college friend, maybe to attend a cooking school or take art lessons, or some such reason. We'd wing it, depending upon how long she needed to be away, which was entirely unclear when she left. But in Edina, as in most neighborhoods, everyone seems to know everything. Maybe Jenna told someone in confidence, who told someone else in confidence . . .

On the phone, Susan told me that the Tanner family was in her prayers, and that, if I ever needed anything, anything at all, I should just let her know—let *her* know, not her and Henry. Or maybe I was just imagining an inference that wasn't intended.

I wasn't. That night, at dinnertime, the doorbell rang and there was Susan holding a casserole dish covered with aluminum foil, saying it was a tuna hot dish. "Lutheran penicillin," she joked. Susan is an attractive woman in her early forties with shoulder-length blonde hair, blue eyes, and a very nice body. She was wearing a tight midriff-baring tee shirt and white tennis shorts.

Susan had sort of flirted with me over the years, in that lighthearted, nonspecific way that seems to say, I'm noticing you, you're in the cohort of men who, under the right circumstances, might interest me. I did the same with certain women, and I assumed Jenna did, too, with some men in our social circle. I didn't imagine that most people ever meant to go beyond mere flirtation; it was just a form of hardwired mating behavior without any real mating intended. Of course, there were (and are) affairs in Edina, just like everywhere on the planet, but I didn't actually know of any in our circle of friends. Maybe Jenna did and didn't mention this to me.

Now here was Susan Toth on my doorstep. I knew I'd come to one of those life-altering forks in the road which life presents to us all from time to time. Should I thank Susan for the casserole and say good evening, or invite her into the house? Jenna and I hadn't had sex since Hope disappeared. But without knowing exactly why—loyalty to Jenna, shyness, performance anxiety because I'd been out of the game for a while, all of the above—I took the casserole and said, "This is so nice of you Susan. How's Henry?" Knowing that the mention of her spouse was unmistakable code for thanks, but no thanks.

Susan handed me the dish, kissed me lightly on the mouth and said, "Enjoy. Do let me know if you need anything else, Jack."

As I watched her walk to her car, and give me a smile and a wave as she got in, I recalled an article in a magazine, maybe *GQ* or *Men's Health*, that said men have an average of X sex partners in their lives and women have an average of Y. I didn't remember the numbers, but did recall that Y was considerably greater then X. My X was six. I never asked Jenna about her Y.

I channel-surf to CNN. Wolf Blitzer, who showed Jenna and me kindness and sensitivity during our appearance on his program, has a report about a college boy in Minnesota who disappeared while walking home from a party, one of four such disappearances over the past two years. Jenna and I knew about the others, and felt badly for their families in a distanced sort of way.

Will Wolf mention the similar case of Hope Tanner? I wonder. He does not. That's old news by now, a thought that saddens me.

I turn off the TV and locate tiny bottles of Scotch in the minibar, reflecting that I am grossly overpaying for the alcohol, but I need a stiff drink. Hope is still missing and almost certainly dead. Jenna is in residence at The Sanctuary. And, distracted by all of this, and grieving myself, I've been unable to focus on anything, including my job. When my law firm had to begin "downsizing" as clients slashed budgets for outside legal counsel because of the recession, the management committee shocked me by putting my name on the hit list. My billable hours were consistently below the minimum expected of a partner. A month ago, I was unceremoniously fired. Before the recession, you never heard about law firm partners being fired, except in extreme circumstances, such as violating the morals clause in their partnership agreement. I can't say I would have voted any differently about another partner in the same circumstance as mine.

It's nearly six o'clock. I use my cell phone to call *Chief* Douglas to confirm our dinner. I'm transferred through three levels of gatekeepers, explaining my business to each one, before being put through to Vernon, a sign of his high office. We have a brief, cordial chat. I don't ask about the case of Hope Tanner because I know that if anything were new, he'd have called me immediately.

Then I speed dial Pete Dye, the private investigator Hartfield, Miller employs whenever the need arises in service of our (now their) clients. "Pistol Pete" the lawyers call him, because of the big black .45-caliber pistol he wears, visible in a black leather shoulder holster when his suit coat flaps open.

"I'm a partner in the firm of Smith & Wesson," he sometimes says, joking but not joking, I think. In my opinion, showing his gun is a marketing tool, meant to communicate the message that he is a serious player in the shadow world of investigation he inhabits. It must work, because Pete's hourly billing rate is equal to that of a senior partner.

Pete is an ex-marine, and former Minneapolis police detective. He works out of a small office above a clothing store in downtown Saint Paul. I've been there many times since Hope disappeared, employing him myself. The office is right out of a Sam Spade movie: a battered oak desk with two leather club chairs pulled up in front, a bookcase containing a surprisingly eclectic collection of volumes about art, history, psychology, and other academic subjects, along with crime novels by John Sandford, Michael Connelly, Lee Child, Bruce DeSilva, Chris Knopf, and other authors. I shouldn't have been surprised, but was, to learn that Pete Dye graduated from Cornell University.

I hired him to supplement the police investigation into Hope's disappearance. When the official investigation wound down without result, I changed his assignment to providing periodic reports on the whereabouts and activities of Slater Babcock, whose father, Pete learned, had more than once bought his son's way out of juvenile-delinquent, spoiled-rich-kid sorts of trouble. At the University of Wisconsin, Pete told me, the only items on Slater's "rap sheet" were participating in the kidnapping and head shaving of a rival school's lacrosse captain (Slater played varsity midfielder), covering trees at the headmaster's house with toilet paper during one exam week, and allegedly taking part in the break-in of a history profes-sor's office in search of exam questions. It's a big leap, Pete emphasized, from stuff like that to murder.

Once it became clear that Slater would not be charged with any crime related to Hope's disappearance, Pete reported, he dropped out of school and spent a few months traveling in Europe, then settled in Key West, where daddy bought him a bar and a house.

"I'm not convinced that Babcock is responsible for Hope's disappearance," he told me. "Of course, there's a first time for everything. A murderer isn't a murderer until his first kill. Even if Babcock is responsible, maybe it was a mistake, some sort of accident, a drug overdose or alcohol poisoning from binge drinking, that harmed Hope, and caused Babcock to panic and cover it up until he was in too deep to admit it. Not that this would excuse his behavior. But you've got to understand that we might never find out what happened that night, unless Babcock, or someone else, finds Jesus and confesses."

"The police have no other suspects," I said, a fact he, of course, already knew.

"True. But they didn't have enough to arrest him, so there's nothing we can do about him except keep track of his location and activities, as I'm doing. If he's really a bad guy, he'll do something else, they always do, and I'll find out. Then we'll have him."

After Hope's disappearance, while her story was still big news, well-intended citizens and cranks had called the Madison Police Department with Hope sightings all over the country and the world. She was seen walking with a man in a mall in Cleveland, apparently willingly. She was spotted at LAX boarding an overseas flight with a man wearing sunglasses and a trench coat who was gripping her arm tightly, and she seemed drugged. A couple vacationing in Gstaad saw her alone on a ski lift just ahead of them, then taking off down a double black diamond slope. Hope did not ski.

Pete ran down the few leads that had some chance of validity, finding all of them to be false. One involved a psychic with a nationally syndicated radio show who said she knew positively that Hope had been abducted by a South American crime cartel that sold girls into sex slavery. Hope had been taken and was now in a brothel on the Caribbean island of Curaçao, the psychic claimed. She had managed to call the radio show, collect, from a pay phone. How Hope got the phone number was not explained. The tape of this call was aired repeatedly for two weeks, which just happened to coincide with a network ratings period. On the tape, a young woman's voice, barely audible through static and her sobbing, seemed to say, "Oh God please help me, help me mommy and daddy, they're hurting me . . ."

I knew my daughter's voice, and that was not it. But at Jenna's insistence, and with my reluctant approval because of my wife's delicate mental state, Pete flew to Curaçao and toured the brothels. He did not find Hope, but he did locate a sixteen-year-old girl who had gone missing from her bedroom in the middle of the night two years earlier in Fort Collins, Colorado. Her stepfather was a suspect in her disappearance.

Pete, posing as a customer, examined the brothel's lineup of girls, and remembered that girl from photos of her that were shown on TV news programs and printed in the newspapers. Instead of shooting his way out with her, he offered the proprietor ten thousand dollars cash from his wallet for the girl. Sold. The girl's father reimbursed Pete, of course. After that, Pete himself was on all the talk shows, which was very good for business.

"Hello, Jack," Pete says, answering on the first ring.

"Hey Pete. Just checking in."

"From where?"

"Does it matter?"

I've called him from the office, from home, and while I was on business trips all over the country, but he'd never asked my location before.

"Your house is all buttoned up, your car is in the garage, no one seems to know where you are. At least no one I'm in touch with. I'm just curious about what's up."

Pete surely knows I was fired from Hartfield, Miller, but is diplomatic enough not to mention it. He can probably guess where I'm heading. That's his job and he's good at it.

"I'm not paying you to watch *me*," I say, a bit annoyed.

"I always like to know what's going on with my clients," Pete answers. "That is what you pay me for."

"Okay. I always wanted a motorcycle. So I bought one. I'm just taking a little ride to break it in."

"A motorcycle. What kind?"

"A Harley-Davidson Road King."

"You should have asked me," Pete says. "I've been riding cycles since I was a kid. I would have told you that Japanese is the way to go. I've got a Kawasaki KX100 that I ride off-road up in the north woods. Motorcycle mechanics fix Harleys and drive rice burners."

"I just liked the look of the Road King," I say, a bit defensively.

"Well, it doesn't have to last forever, does it? Just for this one trip."

"What?"

"We've talked about this, Jack," Pete says. "About you not doing something stupid, especially after all this time. I think you're riding a goddamned Hog to Key West, to do exactly *what* when you get there? *If* you get there."

"Maybe we shouldn't be talking about this," I tell him. Private investigators are required to report to the police any criminal activity on the part of their clients, or any knowledge that a crime may be committed. I don't know if I'm actually planning a crime, but I don't want to put Pete in an awkward position with the law. Or to be prevented from reaching my destination.

"Look, Jack, go home and let me go to Key West, if that's where you're headed," he says. "What'll you do, hit the kid with your briefcase? Turn him in to the IRS for not reporting tips at his bar? I can go there, talk to him, maybe tell him I've uncovered some evidence of his involvement in Hope's disappearance that the police don't know about. Hope's family just wants to know for certain what happened to her, I'll tell him. Wants to know more than they want you prosecuted."

That's not a bad plan. In fact, it's a very good plan. But I'm convinced that I must face Slater Babcock myself, or I'll never find any peace of mind, if peace of mind is even a possibility for me now. I don't just need to find out about what happened to my daughter, I need to be the one finding out. So, after grieving for the past year, and inwardly raging, and being paralyzed by indecision like Hamlet, and helplessly watching Jenna consumed by sorrow, I'm finally taking action, the action being attempting to navigate an eighteen-thousand-dollar motorcycle from my home in the Minneapolis suburb of Edina, to Key West, Florida, the southernmost tip of the continental United States: Land's End, where you either hit the brakes or get wet. Finally, I felt that I had to confront Slater Babcock. I simply cannot ignore the possibility that he might have been involved, or at least know more than he was admitting to the police. I'm convinced that I have to at least try to find out what he did or what he knows, or I'll be in residence at The Sanctuary, too.

Packing for the trip, I found the Browning .380 semiautomatic pistol in my dresser drawer at home, which I bought years ago for home security and have never fired. I considered taking it with me but decided that learning how to operate one mechanical device was enough.

"I'll check in with you later," I tell Pete. "I'm in Madison meeting an old friend for dinner."

"That would be Vernon Douglas," Pete says. "Don't tell him where you're going. He won't like it any more than I do."

"Roger that," I say, using military lingo I picked up from him.

"Stay safe," Pete says. "Check in with me whenever you want to." And we end the call.

Ever since Hope disappeared and I decided that her boyfriend was responsible, I've had all the thoughts I suppose any father would have about what to do under such circumstances: kill Slater Babcock myself, or hire a hit man, or hire someone to torture him until he confesses . . . But law-abiding citizens like me, like most of us I think, only imagine such actions.

I remembered the case of Natalee Holloway, who disappeared on her high school graduation trip to Aruba, never to be found. Circumstantial evidence pointed to a young man named Joran van der Sloot, but he was never arrested; five years later he pleaded guilty in Peru to the murder of a Peruvian woman on the fifth anniversary of Natalee's disappearance and was given a twenty-eight-year prison sentence. I recall thinking back then that, if I were Natalee's father, I would extract vigilante justice. But now it's my daughter who has disappeared, and I haven't done any of the things I imagined any father would.

My neighbor, Hank Whitby, owns an insurance agency. He is in his fifties, balding and somewhat overweight. He does not look like the warrior he was in his youth and, it turns out, still is. He served as an army platoon leader in Vietnam. When a burglar made the mistake of entering the Whitby home at three in the morning six years ago, Hank came downstairs in his boxer shorts and put three rounds from his service revolver into the burglar's chest, killing him.

The deceased perp turned out to be a career criminal with no history of violent acts, unarmed except for a Swiss Army knife. Nevertheless, the Edina police detective investigating the incident, a Vietnam vet himself, found the shooting to be a justifiable homicide, and no charges were filed. The *Minneapolis Star Tribune* noted that Minnesota is one of the states with a "castle law," which gives a person wide latitude in defending his home from an intruder. All letters to the editor that the paper printed after the shooting agreed that the burglar had it coming. An editorial stopped short of saying that, but did strongly support the state's castle law and the Second Amendment.

So what would Hank Whitby do if his daughter were harmed, and he knew, or thought he knew, who did it? I believe that Hank would relentlessly track down the suspect and, if convinced of his guilt, serve as judge, jury, and executioner. Or at least find a way to determine for certain that the suspect was not involved.

So finally, having lost everything that matters to me, I'm on my way to Key West, hoping that the journey will somehow be transformative. I can no longer tolerate being the kind of man who trusts the law, or fate, to deal with the evil in the world when it appears on his own doorstep. I must somehow lose my civility, and become more like Hank, or as close to him as a guy with my résumé gets, when I arrive. If this doesn't work, then I'm lost, and Jenna along with me.

A fool's errand? Maybe. I'll find out when I run out of road.

7

At seven P.M. I walk into the Timber Lodge Steakhouse, located on Highway M on the northwest shore of Lake Mendota. Vernon Douglas and I have dined here before. I find him sitting beneath a stuffed moose head, in a booth near the back of the dining room.

"I suppose I should salute you now," I say as I hang my leather jacket on a hook and slide into the booth.

Vernon shrugs as he half rises to shake my hand, saying, "Oh, yeah. The chief thing."

"That's very nice for you, Vernon. You've certainly earned it."

"Yes," he replies as he takes a sip from his mug of beer. "I do believe I have."

Vernon has been with the Madison PD for eighteen years and is its first African American chief. He was a detective with the Chicago Police Department before that. Early on, I asked Pete Dye to check out Vernon's background. Pete's assessment: Vernon Douglas is a good man and a first-rate cop.

The waitress arrives to take my drink order. I tell her I'll have a martini with three blue-cheese olives. Usually, I'd order a beer, or maybe the house red. But this is the new Jack Tanner—or at least a man in search of the new me. So I order what Hank Whitby always gets when we've been to dinner together. Maybe it's some sort of manly elixir.

Over drinks and steaks, Vernon says he likes the pay and other perks of the chief's job, but gets bogged down by the heavy administrative duties that keep him from doing what he loves, which is making bad guys wish they'd never come to Madison.

I say that I'm taking some vacation time, not mentioning that it is a permanent vacation.

"I've decided to recharge my batteries by riding a motorcycle to Virginia to see Jenna, who's visiting her sister there," I explain. "Then we'll ride back to Minnesota together."

Liars, in an attempt to seem convincing, always provide too much detail, a fact that Vernon Douglas knows as well as anyone on the planet. But he lets it slide. We chat about the Badgers and Packers, about the harsh winter, and other such mundane subjects. Then I clearly startle him—and myself—by asking, with an attempt at nonchalance, "I was wondering, Vernon, if you've ever had to shoot someone."

He sighs as he cuts a piece of steak.

"I'm not going to ask why you want to know that," he says. "Most cops never fire their weapons, other than on the range."

He pauses while he chews the piece of steak and downs the last of his beer, then continues.

"As a rookie cop in Chicago, I responded to a report of shots fired in Cabrini Green, the housing project that's been torn down. Everyone rolling responds to a call like that, but I was a block away and got there first. I saw someone lying on the sidewalk and a young man standing over him, holding a pistol. As I roared up, lights and siren, the guy turned toward me and fired at my cruiser, shattering the windshield. I rolled out the door onto the ground and ordered the guy to surrender. You know, they never seem to follow that order during a gun battle. He fired again. I returned fire and hit him with three rounds center mass, killing him."

He shakes his head, a look of sadness on his face.

"He was only fifteen years old. But there was nothing else I could do."

Then Vernon gives me a look that manages to be hard and sad at the same time.

"Still, you don't forget something like that, ever. Unless you're one of those psychopath flatliners with fucked-up brain chemistry."

He looks up at the moose head on the wall.

"I wouldn't even want to shoot that fellow, if I didn't have to. Although, obviously, someone felt differently."

I check my watch. It's nine o'clock.

"I need to get some sleep, Vernon. I want to get on the road early, out ahead of rush hour."

I insist on picking up the check, in honor of his promotion. We walk out to the parking lot, where he admires the Harley.

"I guess this'll get you wherever it is you're going," he says.

"As I said, Vernon, I'm going to visit Jenna in Virginia."

"Uh huh, sure you are." He grabs my arm, so hard it hurts. "Listen, you're a good guy and you don't deserve what happened to your family." He lets go and shakes his head. "What's it like to *shoot* someone? Jesus, Jack. What'd you do, track that kid down and now you've suddenly grown the cojones for some vigilante justice? Don't go there. Don't go anywhere near there. Look, I hate it that the perp, whoever he is, Slater Babcock or someone else, is out there somewhere, but . . ."

I mount the saddle and say, "What would *you* do if someone killed your daughter and got away with it?"

"Probably hunt down the scumbag, shoot him in the kneecap just to get his attention, and then do some really bad things to him."

I start the Harley.

"That's what I thought."

I ease the cycle off its stand, rev the engine, and pull away, gravel crunching under the tires. I can see in the rearview mirror that Madison Police Chief Vernon Douglas is saying something, but I can't hear him above the growl of the engine.

8

After eight hours, I've ridden as far as my aching body will allow today, and then some. I now have a greater appreciation for the comfort of the luxurious cockpit of my BMW. I check the digital clock below the cycle's speedometer: seven P.M. I'm on I-70 heading east, approaching Columbus, Ohio. I need gas, a meal, and a hotel. I motor down the highway for fifteen more minutes, then lean onto the exit ramp for Grandview Heights, a Columbus suburb. Ohio State University is in Columbus. That was one of the schools Hope considered. If only she'd chosen Ohio State, or anywhere but the University of Wisconsin.

I roll into a Citgo station. As I fill the tank, I think about that crisp October afternoon, the leaves in full fall color, reds, oranges and browns, when Hope and I drove twelve and a half hours from Edina for a campus visit, on the same route I've just taken. Hope insisted on sharing the driving, saying, "You're no spring chicken anymore, daddy," and this phrase became a running joke in our family.

OSU is one of those lovely Midwestern state universities, its imposing campus exuding a mix of wholesomeness and high purpose, students and faculty strolling across the quad as they discuss the nineteenth-century Lake Poets, or string theory, where to get the best pizza, or the football team's prospects for the new season.

Hope noticed that everyone she met insisted on calling the place *The* Ohio State University, which she found a bit pretentious. "I don't know if I can do that all my life," she said.

"Maybe I should go someplace else." When I didn't immediately respond, she added, "Just kidding, dad."

Hope was admitted to the University of Wisconsin, Ohio State, the University of Minnesota, and the University of Michigan. Everywhere she applied. She was very methodical in her criteria: stay in the Midwest, strong academics, not too long a drive from home, big campus with lots of activities in a nice university town.

She picked Wisconsin because it fit all her criteria perfectly. Anywhere was fine with Jenna and me, as long as Hope was happy with her choice. But if she'd happened to choose Michigan, my alma mater, well, I was a big college football fan and Hope could have gotten student game tickets whenever we visited Ann Arbor during the season. I didn't mention this perk while she was making her decision or afterward.

At Edina High School, Hope was an excellent student. She played lacrosse, edited the student newspaper, and was Queen of the Junior Prom. She was friendly, charming, and lovely, with blue eyes and blonde hair like Jenna, and always had a boyfriend. They were all nice young men, as far as I could tell; Jenna and I knew their parents. I don't know if any of them were serious relationships. In my high school days, we seemed to have brightly and briefly burning love affairs with no sex. Kids today—is any sentence that begins with "kids today" of any value?—appear to have casual relationships, with sex.

Jenna and I never asked Hope about any of that. We trusted our daughter, and she knew it. During her freshman year at Madison, she did seem to get serious about a senior boy, which made Jenna and me somewhat uneasy because of the age difference. He was the football team's backup quarterback. The boy graduated and joined the marines. He and Hope exchanged letters for a while during her summer vacation. She didn't seem upset when that ended.

Sometime during her sophomore year, she met Slater Babcock.

THE GAS pump's auto shutoff clicks at just under fifteen dollars. The Harley gets fifty-three miles a gallon on the highway. At that rate I'll get to Key West for less than 200 bucks. I turn out of the Citgo and ride toward a Cracker Barrel down at the end of the strip. As I approach the restaurant's crowded parking lot, I notice a roadside sign advertising the "Historic Arcadia Bed & Breakfast" two and a half miles down the road. On an impulse, I decide to check it out.

Jenna always liked to stay in B&Bs on our road trips. I found them to be musty and frilly and overly precious. The proprietors always seemed to be a couple, one or both of whom had dropped out of one kind of rat race or another in favor of the bucolic life running an inn in a converted Victorian house. I don't particularly care for Victorian architecture, antique furniture, lace curtains or shaving in dry sinks. Despite this, all my B&B memories are good ones because pleasing Jenna pleases me.

Exactly two and a half miles down the two-lane blacktop, I come upon the Arcadia, a three-story white Victorian (of course) with purple and green gingerbread trim set in among giant live oak and willow trees, with a back lawn sloping down to a small lake. I guide the cycle along the gravel driveway and stop in front.

There is a porch running along the front of the house. A man is sitting on a bench swing, the rusty chains creaking as he glides back and forth. He appears to be about my age, with a full beard, wearing a red plaid flannel shirt and jeans against the cooling night air. Probably a refugee from the Chicago commodities pits. A golden retriever with a grey muzzle sleeps at his feet. The man nods in greeting as I lean the cycle onto its kickstand, get off, and walk up the porch steps.

"I was wondering about a room for one night," I say as the man rises and offers his hand.

"Garrett Kirkland," he says. "No need to wonder. We've got one available. Got eight rooms here, as a matter of fact, with just three occupied."

He eyes the Harley.

"I've always thought about getting one of those bad boys, but my wife always exercises her veto. Says if I'm having a midlife crisis, I should take up woodworking, or something else that won't kill me. No offense."

"None taken. Can't say she's wrong."

As Garrett takes an imprint of my credit card at an oak rolltop desk in the living room, he explains that he formerly owned a Chicago advertising agency, Kirkland Associates. His wife Marissa was sous chef at Les Nomades.

"Maybe you've eaten there," he says.

"Yes, my wife and I have, many times. It's a favorite of ours."

The charming brick row house on East Ontario Street is in fact one of Jenna and my go-to restaurants when in Chicago. Will we ever dine there again? Do anything together again?

"Maybe you're wondering why two people give up good jobs in an exciting city to own a B&B out here in the boonies," Garrett says.

I nod. It's true.

"Well, when I got an unsolicited offer from a big French advertising conglomerate for a helluva lot more than I thought my shop was worth, I decided to sell. There are no hard assets with an ad agency. The inventory goes down the elevator every night, and your biggest client can call at any time and fire your ass, as happened to me more than once. So, after the wire transfer hit my bank account, I retired. Got bored after a week. We saw a for-sale ad for this place in *Gourmet* magazine. Turned out my wife liked the idea of taking a break from working in someone else's kitchen. That was three years ago."

That is interesting, but I want nothing more at this point than to freshen up and find something to eat; to be polite I ask, "How do you and your wife like it?"

"Absolutely hate it," Garrett answers with a laugh. "We're working harder than we did at our old jobs. Or at least it seems harder because it's mostly boring. We've got the place up for sale and are moving back to Chicago at the end of the month, whether it sells or not. I'll do some marketing consulting. Marissa has lined up a position at Alinea."

Before heading upstairs to my room, I say, "I suppose I missed dinner?"

"Too bad you didn't get here an hour ago," Garrett answers. "Marissa served a nice spread. The guests seemed to enjoy it."

"That's okay. I can go back to the Cracker Barrel."

"Cracker Barrel? No way! Marissa would kill me if I let you do that. She's still in the kitchen. She'll whip up something from the larder. Freshen up and come down whenever you're ready."

Garrett leads me up a creaky wooden staircase to a room on the second floor, insisting on carrying my saddlebags. There is no room key, which is one of a rural B&B's charms, but I have that city dweller's habit of wanting to lock up my stuff. Garrett pushes open the door, flips on the lights, puts the saddlebags onto a webbed suitcase stand at the foot of the bed and departs, reminding me again to come down to the kitchen when I'm ready.

I take in the room, which has a small connecting bathroom. It could be a model for a feature spread in *Bed and Breakfast Business* magazine, which probably does exist; there are specialty magazines for everything. Chintz curtains; lace doilies on every available surface; a four-poster bed with a lace canopy; an antique oak dry sink with a flow-blue bowl and water pitcher. Jenna has a flow-blue collection, which is why I know the term. I wish she was here with me, and that Hope was in school, and we were a family again.

I peel off the leathers, tee shirt, jeans, boots, and the insulated underwear, and stand under a steaming hot shower— unlike many B&Bs the Arcadia has good water pressure—and afterward feel better, physically and mentally. I slip on a white golf shirt, wrinkled from being rolled up in the saddlebags, jeans, and running shoes I brought along, and reflexively look for the nonexistent room key.

I find the back stairway at the end of the hall, which, I assume, will lead me toward the kitchen. As soon as I start down the stairs, I can smell the warm, yeasty aroma of baking bread. If there is a more wholesome, comforting, inviting smell in the world, I don't know what it is.

I follow the aroma down the stairs, along a hallway, and around a corner into the kitchen, which has white walls, black-and-white checked tile on the floor, stainless steel counter-tops, a scarred butcher block, the kind of cast-iron gas range that's always lit, and hanging copper pots that look like they actually get used, unlike the pots in our kitchen, which are for display purposes only.

Marissa Kirkland is bending over in front of the oven, taking out a metal tray holding four bread pans, oven mitts on both hands. She puts the tray on the butcher block, turns, and smiles at me. She is wearing a faded denim shirt, jeans and cowboy boots. Her soft auburn hair falls to her shoulders; she shakes a strand from her face. She is slim and pretty, maybe in her mid- to late-fifties, one of those women who seem to improve with age. I can see threads of silver in her hair and fine lines around her eyes, which are the color of cornflowers. And she can cook. Garrett is a lucky devil.

"Hi there," she says, shaking off the mitts so she can take my hand. "I'm Marissa. You must be Jack. Garrett said you might stop by for a snack."

"That bread smells amazing," I say. "I'd tell you it reminds me of my youth, except our family ate Wonder Bread."

"Sourdough, from starter I brought from Chicago," she tells me as she flips one of the bread pans upside down, taps the bottom with the handle of a chef's knife, slides the loaf out and cuts a thick end slice, which she slathers with soft yellow butter from a dish on the counter.

"Here," she says, handing the bread to me. "I prefer the end pieces. See what you think."

I take a bite. Pure heaven.

"Wow, this is fantastic. It's like I've never tasted bread before."

Marissa seems pleased.

"Pull one of those stools up to the counter and I'll see what I can throw together."

As I perch on the stool, she swings open the refrigerator door and scans the shelves, saying "mmm . . . ah . . . yes . . ." as she pulls out various items, setting them on the butcher block: some field greens in a plastic bag, a red onion, a tomato, something that looks like a withered black mushroom, eggs in a bowl and a brick of yellow cheese.

"We'll do something light, so you can get a good night's sleep," she says as she shakes out the lettuce into a wooden salad bowl. "I think an omelet and green salad will do the trick."

"Sounds perfect," I say, resting my elbows on the counter as she's whisking eggs in a bowl as butter is melting in an omelet pan on a gas burner. The butter is sputtering as she pours in the eggs and uses a grater to add the cheese. She folds the omelet over onto itself, waits a moment, then slides it onto a big white china plate. She spoons some salad onto the plate and grates slivers of the black mushroom onto the top of the omelet.

"Black truffle," she explains. "Gives a cheese omelet a nice finish."

She takes a bottle of red wine from a rack under the butcher block, extracts the cork and pours some into two stemmed glasses. She hands one to me and lifts the other in a toast: "Bon appétit, Jack. A fruity pinot noir, I think, goes well with eggs." She displays the label. "Stag's Leap in the Napa Valley. The vintner's a friend of mine."

She holds the glass to her nose, sniffs, takes a sip, swirls it in her mouth, and swallows. "Very nice. A hint of sassafras, rosemary, and cinnamon, with a light veneer of oak. Mildly assertive, yet not pushy. I'd have to say its presumption amuses me."

I take a sip and shrug.

"Just tastes like a nice red wine to me."

Marissa grins.

"Ha! It tastes like that to me, too! I was just putting you on with that pretentious wine blather. I've seen blind tastings where the so-called experts can't tell the difference between a fifty-dollar French and a ten-dollar California. Or even Two Buck Chuck."

I laugh and dig into my meal with gusto, famished.

"This is wonderful," I tell her.

Marissa cuts another hunk of bread for me, and one for herself, and sits on a stool beside me, spreads butter on her bread and takes a bite. I consider licking my plate. She finds a rhubarb tart in the refrigerator and draws us both little cups of espresso from an antique copper and steel machine she tells me she found in Tuscany.

"So, Jack, if you don't mind me asking, where are you heading on that motorcycle," she says.

Once again, as I did back at the roadside diner, I have the urge to blurt everything out. But this time I think I owe Marissa Kirkland something for the great meal. And, warmed by the meal, the wine, and the company of this interesting and attractive woman, I realize that I am terribly lonely.

Marissa sits silently as I tell it all, every bit of it, feeling a sense of relief, of a burden being lifted from my back, perhaps like a Catholic in the confessional seeking forgiveness for his sins. Jack the blabbermouth. Why burden this nice woman with my personal problems just because she made a nice meal for me?

She stands, gives me a hug, and says, "Oh Jack, bless you, and bless Jenna, and bless Hope. May you all be together again."

I'm deeply moved, and manage to say only, "Thank you."

She begins putting the dirty dishes into the sink, and tells me, "If you're not quite ready for bed you can find Garrett down on the dock. He usually has an extra cigar."

A BRILLIANT moon hangs in the night sky as I make my way along a fieldstone path running down to the lake. The temperature has dropped into the 20s; I'm wearing my leather jacket and a knit cap I brought along. I come to a sand swimming beach. The lake is still frozen. Garrett is seated on a wooden bench, puffing a cigar whose end glows like a firefly in the night. He's wearing jeans, a red plaid lumberjack coat, a Chicago Cubs baseball cap, and cowboy boots.

"Hey Jack," he says. "Join me in a Cohiba?"

I sit on the bench, accept the contraband Cuban cigar, a cutter and box of wooden kitchen matches, snip off the end of the cigar, light it, and take several long draws to get it going. I'm not a cigar smoker, but I have had a few over the years and don't want to refuse Garrett's hospitality.

"The perfect end to a perfect meal," I tell him, adding, "I think I've never eaten so well. Your wife is a fantastic chef."

"They say hunger is the best sauce, but yes, she certainly is that," Garrett agrees, exhaling a long puff of smoke. We enjoy the silence for a while, sitting there under the moon and a blanket of stars. I notice for the first time a little grouping of ice-fishing shacks out on the frozen lake, about fifty yards offshore. When his cigar is down to the yellow and black-checkered band, Garrett stubs it out in a metal bucket full of sand on the ground beside the bench. I hand him mine and he does the same with it.

We stroll back up to the house. I'm feeling a sense of contentment that I haven't felt in a long time, and I'm grateful to the Kirklands for that.

"Sleep well," he says as he opens the screen door for me. "Breakfast's at seven, but feel free to sleep in. Marissa will take care of you whenever you come down."

IN THE morning, I wake early and enjoy a good breakfast with the three couples staying at the Arcadia who are from St. Louis, Cleveland, and Chicago (friends of the Kirklands'). Then I say good-bye on the front porch to Garrett and Marissa, with her giving me a hug and a kiss on the cheek, and I'm back on the road.

So far, this journey has been more about reliving my past life than about new experiences, but I've still got plenty of road ahead of me.

9

What I remember about the accident is cruising along I-70 East, an hour out of Columbus, late morning, under an overcast sky, when a light snow began to fall. The snow was melting as it hit the pavement so the cycle's tires were still getting traction. If I could make it to the next exit, I'd find a motel and wait for better weather.

I turned on my headlight and slowed to ten mph. The Zanesville exit two miles ahead, according to a sign. Fortunately, there was no traffic behind me.

Suddenly, the Harley's rear wheel lost traction, and began to slip sideways, the cycle out of control, heading toward a guardrail. The cycle hit the metal rail and I was airborne, turning ass over teakettle, landing on my back in a frozen farm field.

I remained conscious. I don't remember how long I lay there, feeling no serious pain after I regained my breath, but unwilling to try to get up right away in case I'd broken something. Someone, a passing motorist, must have called 911 because after a while I heard sirens, then saw the flashing lights of an Ohio State Highway Patrol cruiser, which pulled over and stopped. The trooper made his way over the guardrail and through the field, knelt beside me and eased up my helmet visor. "Can you hear me, sir?" he asked.

He looked to be about my age, flecks of grey in his hair, which seemed old for someone still on highway patrol.

"Yes . . ."

"Can you move?"

"Don't know, haven't tried."

"Okay, don't move. An EMS van is on the way."

"My motorcycle?" I asked.

Dumb question. If I'm going to die or be paralyzed, who cares about a motorcycle?

"Looks like it isn't too bad," the trooper said. "We'll attend to it after we get you on the way to the hospital."

The EMS crew arrived; one of the two medical attendants, a young woman, slipped off my helmet, and the other one, a young man, checked my vital signs, and put a brace on my neck. They eased me sideways onto a gurney, and transported me to Muskingum County Hospital in Zanesville, where I was examined, kept overnight, and released the next morning, suffering only from some bruising and a sore back and ribs. I spent the next several hours in a Ramada Inn, taking prescription pain killer pills and soaking in the hotel's hot tub by the outdoor swimming pool. The state highway patrol had arranged for my Harley to be trucked to a mechanic.

To continue or not to continue, that is the question. No one could fault me for abandoning the trip, or at least not continuing it on a motorcycle. No one but me. I realize that this is foolish, but at this point in my life, foolish is what I have left, and rational hasn't been working all that well. The thought of going home, or of arriving in Key West without benefit of the kind of trip I've planned, is simply not acceptable.

I TAKE a taxi from the hotel to Bob's Garage on Adair Avenue in Zanesville. I find Bob, a man in his fifties with a grey crew cut and grease on his hands, in one of the bays working under the hood of a beige AMC Gremlin that looks almost new.

I introduce myself as the guy who owns the Harley. Bob wipes his hands on his coveralls and returns the shake.

"Glad you're up and around already," he says.

He notices that I'm looking at the Gremlin.

"Probably the ugliest car ever made," he says with a grin. "Looks like a pregnant gerbil. It's owned by a farmer who bought it new in '71 for his wife. His wife promptly gave it back to him, so he parked it in the barn, with thirty-two miles on it, the distance from the dealer to home. His grandson found it there and wants it, beats walking I guess, so I've been checking it out for him."

He cocks his head toward a corner of the garage, behind the second bay.

"Your cycle's over there. Let's take a look."

We walk over. My Harley is leaning against the wall, looking . . . sad.

He shakes his head. "You and your bike are lucky some car or truck wasn't coming up on you when it happened. Otherwise, we'd be selling you both for parts."

"I know."

"So, what we have is a bent handlebar, broken foot peg, shattered headlight lens, and broken turn signal, and assorted scrapes and dents. Not too bad under the circumstances. I checked, and I can get the parts from the Harley dealer in Columbus. Owner's a friend. Or, if you'd rather, he can send a truck to take the cycle there for the repairs. Fine with me, either way."

I consider this, then ask, "Have you ever worked on motorcycles before?" Then regret this rude question.

Bob smiles.

"There's a dirt track over by Bloomfield, where they race cycles on weekends. In my younger days, I used to race there. Now, they bring me the broken ones to fix. No Harleys, but I've had a few in the shop, too. But, as I said, I'm fine either way."

The smart thing is probably to have the work done by the Harley dealer. But for some reason, I want to give Bob the business. I like the look of the repair shop, and of Bob. This little rural operation is like something from another age, back when attendants pumped your gas and cleaned your windshield, and people—at least in towns like this one—didn't lock their front doors and left the keys in their cars. In addition to the nostalgia, the factory warranty won't apply.

"I'm good right here," I tell Bob.

"All right then. I'll write up an estimate for your insurance company."

I know that getting an insurance adjuster way out here will take who knows how much time, and I'm eager to get going.

"Just tell me how much and I'll submit the bill to the insurance company later," I say.

"I'd say we're looking at five or six hundred dollars, give or take."

"That's fine. How long will it take?"

"Oh, I can have the parts here later this afternoon, I'll go get them. I'll have it ready by morning, unless I run into a problem."

"Okay, let's do it," I tell him.

"Meanwhile, you can drive my car. I've got the truck."

Bob's car turns out to be a mint-condition 1964 red Corvette convertible, which Bob found in another farmer's barn. These barns are apparently vintage-auto gold mines.

So I stay at the Ramada that night, grateful for the additional time to recover from my aches and pains. When Bob is done, my motorcycle runs perfectly, although, he said, I'd need a body shop to fix the dents and paint job.

Maybe later. For now, I'm back on I-70 East toward Virginia, the weather forecast promising sunny skies all the way.

10

"How's the house, Jack?" Jenna asks as she finds me in the lobby of The Sanctuary's main building in McLean and gives me a kiss on the mouth. Now that I'm in Virginia, the temperature is up in the sixties, so weather is no longer a problem.

"A Ritz-Carleton for head cases," Jenna had termed the hospital when I brought her here just more than eight months ago.

"The house is fine. It'll need painting this summer. It's been six years. The icemaker on the Sub-Zero is broken again, so I'll have to call the repair guy when I get home . . ."

I'm about to tell her something equally mundane about the roof shingles being damaged by the ice and snow when she interrupts me.

"Oh, that's nice," Jenna says. "Did you bring pictures?"

I'm surprised. Jenna has not asked about our house, or about anything else about our life in Edina, since arriving here.

"Sorry, I didn't think of it," I tell her. "I will next time."

At first, I began visiting weekly, flying into Dulles every Saturday and renting a car. But it soon became clear that my visits were upsetting Jenna, and me as well. I hated seeing her in an institution, no matter how nice the furniture was. So I started coming less often, once a month or so. Jenna never seems to care how often I come. At least she hasn't said so.

When we're together I'm reminded that we are childless parents. It must be the same for Jenna too. Hope is never mentioned by either of us. This is the first time I've seen my wife in nearly three months. I understand that the Jenna I'm visiting is a chemically altered version of herself. What saves you changes you. But something seems different today. Is she less tense? The light in her eyes less dimmed? Hard to tell at this point. But something . . . Or am I just imagining this because I want it to be true?

Dr. Kubrick, Jenna's staff psychiatrist, has counseled me that, in time, she will want to talk about the reality of our situation, and this will signal substantial progress on the road to healing. But we shouldn't rush it.

How long will that take? I asked. Dr. Kubrick couldn't say. Each person is unique. Kind of like being in a coma: sometimes all we can do is wait and hope for the best. Which made me wonder why Jenna couldn't wait it out at home, seeing her psychiatrist there as an outpatient, instead of here at a cost of ten thousand dollars a month, with insurance covering less than half that amount. But she clearly wants to be here, so we're making it work. On the one hand, money should be no object. On the other, it will be, if we run out. I'm out of work and soon must pay our health insurance premiums. I don't know how much longer we can afford for Jenna to be here. Nothing to do now but wait and see.

It's four o'clock. Jenna is wearing her usual Sanctuary garb: a tennis warm-up suit, this one, pink velour, and running shoes. Exercise is a big part of the treatment here. Jenna does yoga and Pilates, and takes long walks around the grounds.

I'm trying to think of more to report about life at home, anything but the fact that I won't be returning there when I leave her, at least not directly, when Jenna announces, "They're serving tea in the conservatory. I love those little cucumber sandwiches, and the pastries. Lately I can't seem to resist the sweets."

Another first.

She loops her arm through mine and leads me down a hallway with marble floors and oil paintings on the walls, some by artists whose names I recognize. I can't help thinking that we're paying for them. The hallway feeds into a large, sunny room with full-length windows looking out onto the manicured grounds of an English estate garden.

The conservatory has more art on the walls, plus antique furniture—I'm guessing the pieces are not reproductions—and mahogany floor-to-ceiling bookcases. They do not call this the "day room," I decided during my first visit, because that would bring to mind prisons, nursing homes, and low-rent mental institutions. The Sanctuary is anything but low rent.

Twenty or so other visitors and patients—patients are called "guests" here—are snacking from a long banquet table covered with a white tablecloth. Jenna has put on some weight, I notice, but she still looks beautiful despite this, despite it all.

My lovely, loving, damaged Jenna.

She leads me to the buffet table where we fill our plates with various crustless sandwiches and miniature pastries. Jenna pours tea for herself and coffee for me, remembering my beverage preference, while having suppressed so much else of greater importance.

"This is nice," Jenna says when we're seated in uphol-stered chairs near a window, plates balanced on our knees and our cups on a mahogany butler table with brass hinges. "I'm glad you came."

She looks at me, seeming concerned.

"You look tired, Jack. I hope you didn't drive all the way here from Minneapolis without stopping overnight."

Which would have been more than eighteen hours, straight through. And why does she think I drove instead of flew, which I've always done?

"I stayed in Milwaukee and Columbus," I tell her, not wanting to mention Madison.

I am fatigued, and dinged up like the Harley. I feel as if I've ridden here on a horse. I've never ridden a horse, but this must be what it feels like when you're done with a long ride, at least if you're a tenderfoot like me. The first day on the Harley was exhilarating, adrenaline masking any discomfort. The second day, eight hours in the saddle to Columbus, reminded me why they invented automobiles. Then the accident. And today I rode seven more hours to McLean.

We continue to chat amiably for another half an hour, discussing the pleasant Virginia climate, the new wing under construction at The Sanctuary, where Jenna is in line for a larger suite when it's completed (at an increased cost), the new chef who has added lighter spa cuisine to the menu, the chaperoned outings you can take to shopping malls and movies and plays, blah blah blah, as we sip our tea and coffee and eat our sandwiches and pastries. Again, I think that Jenna seems more connected than during my previous visits.

She startles me by asking, "Did you also stop in Madison?"

At a loss, I tell her an edited version of the truth.

"I did. I was tired, so I found a hotel . . ."

"Did you see the campus?"

"I drove through it," I admit.

"Okay," Jenna says, and, to my relief, is done with this subject.

When I check my watch, she surprises me again by saying, "Why don't you come up to my room and rest up a bit before leaving."

I've been to her room only twice before, when she moved in and again when I brought her some things from home she requested: certain clothing, her cosmetics case, her sewing kit (a birthday gift from Hope, which she's never used) and her laptop computer.

Every other time, we've met in the conservatory and then walked the grounds, or had lunch or dinner in the dining room, depending upon the time of day. Maybe Jenna considers her room to be her personal sanctuary. I've never asked to go there because I didn't want to upset whatever delicate balance might be helping her survive.

Jenna is free to leave the hospital grounds whenever she wishes, either on an excursion, or permanently. Once, at her request, I took her to a nearby outlet mall. She bought a hair dryer, some pajamas, and new jogging shoes, and we had lunch. It was nice, but she hasn't wanted to venture out again, at least not with me.

Her room is actually a spacious and well-appointed apartment, with a living room, bedroom, small kitchen, and a breakfast nook. She leads me into the bedroom, turns down the comforter and sheet on the canopied bed, and says, "I think a shower and a nap before leaving is what you need."

For me, this is an unexpected but welcome prospect before hitting the road again. I undress as Jenna watches, toss my clothes onto the bed, go into the bathroom, adjust the showerhead to pulsate, let the hot water massage my neck, shoulders and back, use a loofah sponge for a nice scrub, and then wrap a big terrycloth towel around me and pad back into the bedroom.

Jenna is under the covers, smiling, her blonde hair fanned out on the pillow. I drop the towel, slide under the covers and embrace my beautiful wife, who is also nude. She kisses me and says, "I've been missing you."

I'm overwhelmed with emotion. The old Jenna has reappeared, it seems, at least for this brief time.

The visit becomes conjugal. Lost in the moment, the past is held in abeyance, the future is irrelevant, there is only the sweet present time, a feeling I'd almost forgotten. Later, Jenna lies in bed watching me pull on my shirt, pants, and motorcycle boots. Time to go. She looks happy.

She sits up and shakes a strand of hair from her eyes, a Jenna thing.

"So, cowboy, you just ride into town, steal a lady's heart, and then ride out again. Is that the deal?"

I study her and decide to go for it.

"Do you want me to take you home?"

"You mean ride to Minnesota on the back of that motorcycle? Like I'm your biker bitch?"

So she saw me arrive. She must be able to see the parking lot from her window. I hadn't remembered that. I laugh. This really is the Jenna I've always known.

"Sure, if you want. Or we can fly, or rent a car, or buy a car, whatever you like."

She sighs and looks away.

"I can't do that, Jack. Not yet. But don't give up on me. Don't give up on us."

Out in the parking lot, the night illuminated by sodium-vapor lights, I start up the motorcycle. As I buckle my helmet, I look up at the window of Jenna's suite. She is standing there, backlit, in a white terrycloth robe, waving at me. I wave back. Then she places her palm upon the window glass, as if touching the night.

I push the Harley off its kickstand, turn my hand on the throttle and cruise away, wondering if Jenna is coming back to me, or if I just took a nap in her room and all the rest was a sweet dream.

11

At seventy miles per hour there is no way for two people on a motorcycle to talk, unless they have helmets with a wireless intercom system. I have just one helmet, and it isn't rigged like that anyway because I hadn't planned on a passenger.

All I know about the young, pretty, red-haired, green-eyed girl sitting behind me with her arms around my waist is what she told me when I spotted her hitchhiking at the entrance ramp to I-95 South in Fredericksburg, where I spent the night after leaving Jenna.

Her name is Hannah. She is from Fargo. She is eighteen, but I wouldn't have been surprised if she'd said thirteen. She is wearing plastic Minnie Mouse sunglasses, a tight Jonas Brothers tee shirt, skimpy cutoff blue jean shorts called Daisy Dukes, I know from Hope, and pink flip-flops. I'm south of the Mason-Dixon Line now; the temperature is in the low 60s and I'm wearing jeans and a tan poplin golf jacket with an Edina Country Club logo over a blue work shirt. My leathers are rolled in my saddlebags, and I don't expect to need them again on this trip.

Hannah was riding on the back of her boyfriend's motorcycle, another Harley, from Fargo to Daytona Beach for Bike Week, she told me when I stopped. She and the boyfriend had a fight over "whatever," and he dumped her back at a Days Inn. She still wants to get to Daytona. Am I headed that way?

I decided on the spot that I would make an unplanned stop in Daytona. It might be an interesting adventure. At least that's what I told myself. "Hop aboard, Hannah," I said, and patted the saddle behind me. "Sorry, I don't have another helmet."

"Never wear one," she answered. "Gives me helmet hair."

She swung up onto the rear seat and shouted, "Giddyap horsey!" And off we went.

I feel her tapping my shoulder. We've been riding for nearly two hours, heading south down I-95 toward Richmond. I swivel my head and see her pointing at a sign announcing a highway rest area coming up in two miles. I nod and give her a thumbs-up, swing into the rest area and park in front of a one-story red brick building that looks like a small elementary school. Semis, pickups, and campers are parked in a designated truck area. As I dismount, I notice a group of motorcycles parked several rows back. I pull off my helmet and jacket as Hannah hops off, grinning.

"Sure has warmed up," she says, tugging down her tee shirt, which has ridden up to reveal the bottoms of her breasts. The denim Daisy Dukes leave very little to the imagination.

Bad dog (me). But I can't control what I think, only what I do, and I certainly don't plan to do anything with this girl except give her a lift to Daytona.

A portly, silver-haired, older woman getting into the passenger side of a Hyundai in the next space over is glaring her disapproval at me, which makes me wonder—theoretically—what the age of consent is in whatever state we'll end up in tonight. Or maybe the old bat just doesn't like motorcycles.

Hannah crinkles her nose and says, "Boy, thanks for stopping. I sure gotta pee, don't you?"

"Morning coffee goes right through me," I admit.

"You go first and I'll watch the cycle," she says. She indicates the saddlebags with a nod. "I mean, these aren't locked on or anything, are they?"

"Okay," I tell her.

I had two big mugs of coffee with breakfast at the Fredericksburg Ramada Inn. One of my law partners, discussing the challenges of aging, quipped that you can tell a man has passed a milestone when frequency and urgency refer to urination and not sex. Got that right.

"Hey, I was just thinking," Hannah calls out as I'm walking toward the building. I stop and look back. "We could save some money if we got just one hotel room tonight."

Interesting. Of course, I won't take her up on it; I'll pay for a second room. But the novel *Lolita* does come to mind. A sexy young girl like Hannah surely can have any man she wants, so I wonder why she's flirting with an old coot like me. Maybe she's just amusing herself.

Inside the building, I pass vending machines and a wall containing a big highway map of Virginia, turn into the men's room, and find myself standing at a urinal beside a man in his fifties, wearing a denim jacket with the sleeves cut off. The back of the man's jacket reads "Devil's Disciples," with a grinning devil's head beneath the ornate script. He must be one of the motorcycle gang from the parking lot.

As we're at the sink washing our hands, I notice in my peripheral vision that he is wearing a golf shirt under the open jacket, jeans with a pressed-in front crease, along with boots like mine. No visible tattoos. He certainly doesn't fit my idea of an outlaw of the open road. He gives a friendly nod, dries his hands with a blower, and leaves first.

I walk outside and look around. I can't see Hannah or the Harley. The building has two fronts, each facing a parking lot, so I must have gotten turned around. I walk through the open center atrium of the building and scan the front row on the other side. Still no Hannah or Harley. What's up with this? I notice that there is no truck-parking area on this side, so it must have been the other side where I parked.

I go back through the building and over to the place where I think I left Hannah and my cycle. There is one empty space. I get a feeling like you do when you've misplaced your wallet or cell phone, or car keys, but worse. I've somehow misplaced a girl and a motorcycle. Did I leave the key in the ignition? I pat my pockets. Not there. Maybe Hannah couldn't wait for me, and went to the ladies room, leaving the key, and someone drove off with my motorcycle. When she comes out, I won't be angry, it was an honest mistake. Insurance will cover the loss.

I wait five minutes or so, and she doesn't come out. I go inside to the ladies room entrance, thinking to call out her name. Instead, I stop a middle-aged woman on her way in.

"Excuse me, sorry to bother you," I tell her. "I'm looking for my daughter. Would you mind seeing if there's a teenage girl inside with short reddish hair, wearing a tee shirt and denim shorts? Her name's Hannah."

The woman looks me over. Maybe she's suspicious about the intentions of an older guy wanting to extricate a teenage girl from a rest stop bathroom.

"She's been in there quite a while, and I'm concerned she might be ill," I explain.

"I suppose I could do that," she finally says, and enters the ladies room. She reappears a moment later. "No one like that in there. Sorry."

Maybe Hannah was kidnapped. I go back out to the rest stop parking area. A boy is holding a leash while a golden retriever sniffs around on the lawn; families are picnicking on benches on a concrete pad under a shelter next to the main building; cars and trucks arrive and depart. Over in the truck lot, a big white, yellow, and green Mayflower moving van roars to life and begins pulling out of its double space. Are Hannah and my Harley in that van, with Hannah tied up and gagged?

While I'm considering running after the van, shouting, it moves away and exits the lot, leaving me wondering what a good next move would be for a guy on foot with no ID, cash, credit cards, or cell phone out here in wherever the hell I am in Virginia. I walk back inside the building and use a pay phone—I didn't know there still were pay phones in this cellular age—to call 911, which doesn't require any coins, then go outside to wait.

No more than fifteen minutes later, a Virginia State Police cruiser pulls up. I walk over and identify myself to the trooper, who's just gotten out of the vehicle, putting on his Smokey Bear hat, just like the trooper in Wisconsin. As we stand beside the cruiser, I tell my sad tale to Sergeant William Bronson, a tall and lean man in his thirties, I'd guess, with a blond crew cut and soft Virginia accent. He listens to the story of a man who should know better than to let himself apparently be scammed by a teenage grifter.

"Need a ride somewhere, Mr. Tanner?" Sergeant Bronson asks after he's taken down all the relevant information in a notebook, including a description of Hannah, No-Last-Name.

I'm about to accept the offer when I notice someone walking toward us from the truck lot. It's the Devil's Disciple guy from the men's room.

"Excuse me, but I saw a girl riding away on a Harley-Davidson, and she threw these over there by the exit ramp," the man says, holding up my saddlebags. "I figured this might be yours, because you're wearing motorcycle boots and talking to the trooper." He has a New England accent.

I rummage around inside the saddlebags, and find my clothing and toilet kit, but nothing else. Who knows why Hannah tossed the saddlebags. Who knows why she stole my motorcycle. Who knows why I picked her up. Was it because she is a hot young Lolita, and I did have some vague sexual fantasy? If so, this is my punishment. My former law partner Ted Berquist used to say, you're only as old as the women you date. Did I really think this girl would want anything more from a fifty-two-year-old man than a ride? Well, apparently Hannah did want more. She wanted my cash, credit cards, cell phone, and motorcycle, and she got them.

"Yes, they're mine, thanks very much," I tell the man.

"I'm sorry about your Harley," he says. He offers his hand. "I'm Harold Whittaker. From Boston."

We shake.

"Jack Tanner, from Minneapolis."

"Do you want a ride, Mr. Tanner?" Sergeant Bronson says with a bit of annoyance in his voice.

"My friends and I are heading to Daytona Beach for Bike Week," Harold says, indicating with a nod a group of five other men standing beside motorcycles. "We can give you a ride there or to the next town, whichever you want."

I don't know what Bike Week entails, but maybe that's where I'll find Hannah and my Harley, so I decide to go with them to Daytona Beach. "I'd appreciate that," I tell Harold.

Sergeant Bronson gives a whatever-floats-your-boat shrug. He reaches into the cruiser and comes out with a business card, which he hands to me. "You can check in with the duty officer to see if we've found your cycle."

"Thanks, I appreciate it," I say as the sergeant gets in the cruiser and drives away.

"Do you know that girl?" Harold asks.

"We just met. She was hitchhiking. I don't even know her last name."

Harold takes a cell phone from his pocket and offers it to me.

"I expect you've got some calls to make. Just come over when you're done. We've got rooms booked in Richmond for tonight. Be happy to stake you to dinner and a room, if you want to go that far."

I power up Harold's cell phone as he walks toward his group. Who to call? Pete Dye, but his phone number is on my cell phone. What about Helen Abelard, the office administrator at Hartfield, Miller? She'd take care of everything, notifying my credit card companies and bank, ordering replacement cards to be FedExed, getting some cash to me, notifying my insurance company, and anything else that needs doing. Even though I don't work at the firm anymore, I've always been pleasant to Helen. Jenna was in charge of sending her a nice Harry & David fruit basket each Christmas, although the last holiday was missed, with Jenna not at home.

I call the law firm's main number and get routed to Helen, who says she's happy to help, no problem at all. She'll track down the info to get the proper authorizations for my accounts.

"We've all missed you," she tells me.

Maybe she has missed me, but probably not my partners, who fired me.

I join Harold and his friends. He introduces me all around: "Jack, this is Tom Jarvis, Alan Dupree, Bill Standish, whom we call Miles, Langdon Lamont, and Victor Purcell."

Tom is tall, with light brown hair and the broad shoulders of a collegiate rower, which, I later learn, he was. Alan is short, pear shaped, with a round face and thinning hair. Miles is bald and wears round wire-rimmed glasses; I imagine that he wears a bow tie to work. Langdon is handsome, tall and lanky, with slicked-back sandy hair and an aquiline nose. Victor is of medium height and has a grey brush cut. All of them wear the Devil's Disciple colors on denim or leather jackets; all are as well groomed as Harold Whittaker; all are pleased to meet me; all have Harold's New England accent except for Langdon, who speaks with a soft Southern drawl.

No one indicates in any way that I'm a naive idiot, which I obviously am. Gentlemen all. I'm wondering what kind of unusual motorcycle gang this is when Harold saves me from asking.

"We're all from the Boston area, except for Langdon, who's from Atlanta and owns a summer place on the Vineyard, where I first met him. I'm an investment banker. Tom is a professor at the Harvard Business School, Alan owns companies, Miles and his wife own a small book-publishing company, Langdon chose the right parents, so he mostly sails and works on lowering his golf handicap, and Vic is a developer of shopping malls."

"I represent that remark," Langdon says, grinning.

"I'm a lawyer, from Minneapolis," I tell them. And then admit, "That was my first motorcycle."

Alan smiles.

"I imagine, with your hourly billing rate, you can buy another one."

I don't mention that I no longer have an hourly billing rate.

"There's a Harley dealer in Richmond," Langdon says. "But as you can see, we prefer other brands."

I check out their rides. All Japanese: a big Honda, two Suzukis, three Yamahas. They all appear to be styled after various Harley-Davidson big-bike models, disguising their Asian provenance nicely: wide and low, with gleaming chrome and fancy paint jobs. The kick-ass Harley look, with Japan's superior technology and fits and finishes. Like a Lexus in Corvette clothing, I think. And like this group of successful professionals masquerading as the Wild Bunch.

"Very nice bikes," I say. "How long have you been riding together?"

"Harold, Alan, and I go back six years," Tom says as he extracts a cigar from his saddlebags, along with a silver cutter and a flip-top Zippo lighter bearing a crimson Harvard crest. He clips off one end, lights up, and takes a long, luxurious drag, the white smoke curling upward as if announcing a new Pope. "The other guys joined us more recently."

"I saw a program about motorcycle gangs on the Discovery Channel," I say. "The Devil's Disciples seemed to be one of the main ones, along with the Hell's Angels, the Outlaws, and some others."

Miles Standish says, "You're wondering how a bunch of WASPy yahoos like us were admitted into one of those highly selective organizations. Like a scholarship kid being tapped for Skull and Bones?"

Langdon grimaces and walks about ten feet away, turning his back to the group.

"I always do that just to piss him off," Miles says. "He's a Yalie and a member of that esteemed club. Whenever you speak its name, a member must leave the room."

Langdon laughs and strolls back over.

"Here's the deal, Jack. I read in *Cycle World*, or maybe it was *American Iron*, that the Disciples decided to cash in on their rep by offering franchises."

"Very high concept," Victor says.

"So I had my lawyer look into it," Alan adds. "Surprisingly, it was legit. Initial franchise fee of ten K, annual dues of one K each, special assessments for things like their legal defense fund. We get to wear the colors, plus we get preferred parking at Daytona Bike Week and Sturgis, and a newsletter with reviews of new cycle models and stories like the best biker bars in Arizona. They even offer discounted motorcycle insurance through GEICO."

"So far, there are eight other franchises around the country," Harold explains. "Langdon suggested it to some friends in Atlanta, and they signed up too."

"There'll be a Disciples hospitality tent at Daytona," Langdon tells me. "We dropped in the first year. We were in fact welcome. Turns out they have a finely tuned sense of irony. You have to love that. But let's just say they party a little harder than we're comfortable with, so now we find our own happy hour."

"How often do you guys go out riding?" I ask.

"Schedules are hard to coordinate," Vic answers. "We get out maybe one weekend a month, cruising to Gloucester for a clam roll or up into Vermont for the fall colors. And then we do this annual ride to Daytona. Langdon is a bachelor. For the rest of us, our wives are mostly understanding, if not fully supportive. 'Boys will be boys,' my wife says, not meaning it as a compliment."

"My wife said, 'sure, go ahead and do your thing, as long as you increase your life insurance,'" Alan says. "So I did."

"There's also a yearly gathering in Sturgis, South Dakota," Vic explains. "But it's too long a ride."

"And the other problem is, when you get there, you're in South Dakota," Tom adds.

His cigar is burned down to the band. He drops it onto the tarmac, stomps it out with his boot, then picks it up and deposits it into a trashcan on the median. Which a real Devil's Disciple probably would not do.

"Time to saddle up," Harold announces. "You can ride with me, Jack. This is a Honda Gold Wing. Heated seat, satellite nav system, heavy-duty suspension, even an air bag. Very comfortable."

Vic chuckles.

"Easy on his hemorrhoids."

Harold takes out a white helmet from under the seat, offers it to me, and then swings up onto the saddle.

"It's my wife's, but it should fit. She likes it roomy so it won't flatten her hairdo on the way to the farmers' market."

"Thanks," I say. "I really do appreciate this."

Mrs. Whittaker's helmet does fit, snugly, but well enough. I find a place to hang my saddlebags, swing myself up, and grip the back of the seat.

Funny, the thoughts you get at moments like this. I remember that the Harley service tech who checked me out on the bike back in Minneapolis told me I'd need to get it serviced after a one thousand mile break-in period. The odometer hit that mark just before I reached McLean, and I'd planned to find a dealer somewhere soon. Now I won't have to. The Road King is such a fine machine that I irrationally hope that whoever ends up as its owner will know to get that service done.

The other guys buckle on their helmets, mount up, and six engines turn over with a sound that is higher pitched than my Road King, wherever it is.

WE ROLL out of the lot, two abreast, Harold and me in the third row, and head back onto I-95 South: six ersatz Devil's Disciples, plus one unaffiliated tax attorney wondering where my own motorcycle is heading, what sort of charges might be appearing on my credit cards, and what new adventures I might find around the next bend in the road.

12

Cocktail hour in Richmond, Virginia, as six motorcycles roll up the brick driveway of the Jefferson Hotel on West Franklin Street and brake to a stop under the broad front portico of the elegant century-old limestone structure.

The finely tuned Japanese engines, sounding like a swarm of locusts compared to the jungle cat growl of my missing Harley, echo under the portico roof. The boys cut them off, lever down their kickstands, and we stiffly ease off the saddles.

Usually, I imagine, the management of a venerable old establishment like the Jefferson wouldn't be pleased by the arrival of a motorcycle gang, even one with reservations. But the Boston chapter of the Devil's Disciples always stays here on the way to Daytona Bike Week, Harold told me this morning as we began our ride. The franchise Disciples, once they have showered off the road dust and dressed up like their real selves for dinner, fit the hotel's target demographic perfectly, he explained. They have made themselves known as gentlemen and generous tippers, so the Jefferson staff is always delighted when they arrive. Their individual preferences are on file in the computer: an extra-firm mattress, a particular brand of mineral water on ice in the room, down or foam pillows, a massage appointment, a six-pack of Sam Adams or champagne or Laphroaig single malt Scotch whiskey. . . . These special needs are always accommodated.

"I trust these digs are acceptable," Harold says to me as he takes a ticket from the valet parking attendant, who has welcomed him back by name. "When we stopped at the battlefield, I called ahead to add you to our group. King bed, pool view. All rooms are nonsmoking."

Tom Jarvis is one of those Civil War buffs who dress in uniforms of the Blue and the Grey for battle reenactments, and who have elaborate setups in their basements depicting troop movements in famous battles. To accommodate Tom's hobby, the Disciples always make a detour on the way to Daytona to the Fredericksburg and Spotsylvania National Military Park for a walk around what historians term "the bloodiest landscape in North America," Tom told me.

I've never studied the subject, but was truly moved by the broad expanse of fields and woodlands where so many young men fell—more than 85,000 wounded and 15,000 killed, the markers said. Numbers so large as to defy comprehension. Compared to this, is the loss of one daughter so tragic?

Yes, it is, to Jenna and me. Catastrophes defy comparison to one another. If you lose someone close, knowing about the carnage of a Civil War battlefield is sad, but of no comfort. Each one of the 100,000 boys and men damaged during that battle had family and friends whose individual grief transcended the general pain of a nation at war with itself. Tremendous numbers of horses were slaughtered too, which saddens me as well.

I ease off my helmet, put my hands on my hips and bend backward with a groan. I'm still not fully recovered from my accident.

"Sounds perfect," I say. "It's been a long day. At this point, I could crash in the lobby."

The valet is a young man dressed as a gentleman who might have roamed the streets of Richmond when Thomas Jefferson was in the White House. As he drives off on Harold's big Honda, two other young men similarly attired swing open the hotel's ornate brass front doors.

Inside the lobby, I take in the soaring ceiling, stained glass skylight, marble columns, hanging tapestries, stone floors, and antique furnishings. Yes, these digs will do nicely after a long day riding as a passenger on the Honda. Jenna would like this place, and Hope, too.

After being shown to my room by a Continental soldier carrying my saddlebags over his shoulder, I collapse into an upholstered armchair, pull off my boots, kick up my legs onto the footstool, and take stock of my situation: here I am in a very nice room with a wood-burning fireplace—the Continental soldier, with my approval, touched off a crackling blaze, requiring the air conditioner to be turned on—in the capital of the Confederacy, with no vehicle, cell phone, cash, or credit cards.

Harold Whittaker kindly gave the desk clerk an imprint of his own credit card to guarantee my payment, and tipped the bellman for me. Like Blanche DuBois, I am depending upon the kindness of strangers.

A bottle of champagne is chilling in a silver bucket on the table beside my chair, which Harold, taking me for a man of refined tastes, must have requested. I take this as a compliment, although I'm more of a beer and wine guy. I pop the cork, pour half a glassful into a crystal flute, take a swig, and review my options.

Thanks to Helen Abelard at Hartfield, Miller, overnight couriers are scheduled to deliver new credit cards in the morning, so I'll be back in business. I'll get a prepaid cell phone from a drugstore. I can find the local Harley-Davidson dealer Harold mentioned and buy a new ride, or maybe find another dealer and switch brands. I like the comfort of Harold's big Honda and the look of the Suzuki and Yamaha, with their rich paint jobs and high-pitched engines that seem to want to run away from the pack. Or I could cab it to the airport, fly to Miami like an adult and rent a car for the drive to Key West. Or rent a car in Richmond. Or book a flight back to Minneapolis, an option always on the table.

I stare into the mesmerizing orange and blue flames and feel their warmth. I remember a snowy winter evening at home in Edina, my family gathered around the hearth when Hope was young, toasting marshmallows in the fireplace. Maybe Hope will suddenly reappear the way those two kidnapped girls did after so many years, what were their names? And then Jenna would be healed, and we'd have our family again.

The ringing of the room telephone interrupts this pleasant fantasy, which, I know, is not going to happen. I push myself up out of the chair, walk over to the desk, and answer.

"Jack, it's Harold. Will you join us for cocktails down in the bar?"

"Sure. Sounds good."

"Great, we're going right down. See you momentarily."

I extract from the saddlebags a pair of rolled-up khaki slacks, along with a green polo shirt, tan V-neck sweater, and my Topsiders. I'll have to go without a sport coat. Setting out, I hadn't packed for cocktail hour with an upscale motorcycle gang in a fancy Old South hotel.

I haven't gotten a haircut in maybe a month, so my hair is longer than usual. I decide that I'll let it keep growing, and also stop shaving. Unsuccessful so far in altering my interior, I can at least change the exterior.

I FIND the boys seated in leather club chairs in the oak-paneled bar, located off the lobby beside the hotel's main dining room. Oil paintings on the walls depict scenes of fox hunting and blue-water sailing. Harold signals to a waitress that we're ready to order drinks. I ask for a beer, the others cocktails or wine, except for Langdon, a Southern dandy of the old school, who wants a Ramos Gin Fizz.

"I like this hotel," I tell them. "Very antebellum. A throwback to a time when Northerners were still welcome in the Old South."

Victor Purcell replies, "And with this recession, our Yankee greenbacks are welcome. I know the owner. He's a big-time real estate developer. Built Hilton Head, among other things."

The drinks arrive.

"No offense, Jack, but . . ." Alan begins.

"Which guarantees that you *are* about to offend," Tom says.

"Point taken. But I was wondering why you chose tax law. It seems rather . . ."

"Arcane?" Tom says. "Boring? No offense, of course."

Everyone is smiling.

"I didn't know what specialty I'd choose when I was in law school," I tell them. "At my law firm, a senior partner is assigned as mentor to each new associate. I drew the head of the tax department, probably because I earned a joint law and accounting degree."

"Smart boy," says Tom, the Harvard Business School professor. "It's all about the numbers."

"I didn't have to choose tax law," I explain. "But the department head was approaching retirement age. He liked me and said tax could be a fast track to partnership. I never regretted it."

Miles Standish, who, I recall, owns a publishing company, stands and raises his glass for a toast. The others all stand too, holding their glasses high. I follow their lead.

Harold explains: "The first year we stayed here, Miles offered a toast with a literary reference, with the challenge that, if we could identify its source, the drinks were on him."

Miles clears his throat.

"Here's to we few, we happy few, we band of brothers!"

"Here, here," they all say, clinking glasses. "To we band of brothers!"

After a moment of contemplation, Alan says, "It's from that book and TV series about a WW Two infantry platoon."

"Band of Brothers," adds Tom.

"Incorrect," Miles says. "These are, of course, the immortal words of King Henry V, put in his royal mouth by the late great William Shakespeare. His St. Crispin's Day speech on the eve of the Battle of Agincourt. Stephen Ambrose did take his book title from the work I cite. So, once again, I've stumped you fellows, which, as you well know, I always enjoy immensely."

WE'RE AT a table in the Jefferson's main dining room, Lemaire, named, the back of the menu explains, for Étienne Lemaire, who served as Thomas Jefferson's maître d'hôtel. White linen tablecloths, crystal glassware, heavy silver utensils and a formally solicitous staff, as befitting Richmond's only AAA Five-Diamond restaurant, according to the menu. The place is full; the other diners are turned out in jackets and ties for the men, and dresses for the ladies. I feel rumpled and underdressed, but no one seems to notice, or, if they do, they don't seem to care.

As we eat and chat, no one mentions the elephant at the table, that being the question: what was a Minneapolis tax lawyer doing on a Harley-Davidson in the company of a young girl at a rest stop off I-95 in Virginia, and why was I so careless that she could steal my motorcycle, wallet, and cell phone? They are too polite to ask.

On top of the glass of champagne in my room, and two draft beers in the bar, I've had my share of five bottles of fine wines served with dinner, and now a snifter of Cognac, quite a bit more than I usually drink. I'm feeling the relaxed warmth of male fellowship, as well as gratitude for their roadside assistance in my time of need.

Although I vowed to tell no one about the purpose of my trip, I did share it with Marissa Kirkland at the Arcadia B&B. These are men of accomplishment and intelligence whose opinions about my situation might be helpful. When there is a lull in the conversation, I say, "Gentlemen, let me tell you a story, and see what you think."

13

Seven motorcycles roll along the meandering band of I-95 South cutting through the farmland and horse pastures of North Carolina: three groups of riders, two abreast, with Alan Dupree alone on point. I'm positioned on the starboard side of the middle group, straddling an Alpine White BMW R 1600 GT purchased with my newly minted Visa card at a dealership on Jefferson Davis Highway just south of downtown Richmond.

I did a Google search of area motorcycle dealers after breakfast at the Jefferson and then made a morning tour of a few of them, browsing brands—Harley, Honda, Yamaha, BMW—with the Disciples, again as a passenger of Harold Whittaker. Everyone enjoyed this and various opinions were offered. I chose the BMW because I liked the look of their bikes and have always had good luck with the company's automobiles. My fellow gangsters voted unanimously for this baby; it even has antilock brakes. The sales kid threw in a tee shirt, quipping, "The tee shirt's twenty-two thousand dollars, the cycle's free."

With my strained finances, the cost of the new motorcycle is a stretch, but I figure I'll apply the insurance money from my stolen Harley and also sell the BMW when the trip is done. I'll ask my agent if I can also file an insurance claim for the repair bill less the deductible.

It's a seven-hour run from Richmond to Savannah, where we'll spend the night. The next day it's a four-hour ride down to Daytona Beach on Florida's Atlantic coast. After I spun out my story over dinner, the boys graciously insisted that they would accompany me to Key West after a shortened stay at Bike Week. They made it clear they are captivated by the righteousness of my mission, by the sense of high adventure, and by their curiosity about what will happen when I get there. I'm certainly curious about that too.

I thanked them, saying we'll talk again about Key West after Bike Week. The truth is I would be glad to have the company the rest of the way, but I'd feel guilty about altering their plans. Only Langdon has been to Key West, they said, and it'd be fun to see. So maybe . . .

Even though we had a big breakfast at the Jefferson, it's nearly two P.M., and I'm hungry. As if he can read my mind, Alan, in the lead, points toward a sign announcing that the Five Aces Truck Stop & Cafe is at the next exit. We follow him down the exit ramp and roll into the restaurant's parking lot.

The only seats available are at a counter in the "Professional Drivers Section," reserved for truckers, whose rank in the hierarchy of motorists calls for them to be segregated from the civilians, like officers from enlisted men at chow time. The Happy Chef back in Wisconsin had that, too.

Tom scans the dining room, shrugs, and leads the way to the counter. Maybe we can pass. We take stools as a waitress brings ice water, fills the coffee cups at our places, hands us menus, and pulls her order pad out of her apron pocket.

"Okay if we sit here?" Harold asks her, in the interest of full disclosure. "We're not truckers."

The waitress smiles. "Figured that. It's fine with me, darlin', if it's fine with those good ol' boys," she answers, nodding toward the other customers in the section, none of them paying attention to anything but their food. We place our orders, and are waiting for our food when a man who must weigh three hundred pounds, seated at the end of the counter, says, loud enough for us to hear, "Well look at that, a buncha queers sitting in the drivers' section." Referring to us, of course, who look like what we are. Pretend truckers and pretend motorcycle gangsters.

The man mountain is dressed in bib overalls with no shirt and has what look to be prison tats on his massive arms: a swastika, a dagger with blue blood dripping off the point, and a Cupid's heart with whatever name was in the center scratched out. His long brown hair is tied back in a ponytail and he has a scraggly ZZ Top beard. I think of the movie *Deliverance*, the "Dueling Banjos" theme song playing in my head.

"If you drop your fork, don't bend over to pick it up," Tom says quietly. He must be thinking of the same movie.

"Bigfoot's got a big mouth," Langdon says. I can't tell if the man heard him.

The waitress moves down the counter refilling coffee cups. When she gets to Bigfoot, he tells her, "I think my meal should be on the house, Hazel, given that these dickheads are makin' me sick."

Hazel shrugs and goes into the kitchen. Bigfoot finishes his meal, picks up his check and, as he passes us on his way to the checkout counter, says, "Sure hope I don't run over any motorcycles on my way out of the lot."

Langdon slides off his stool, follows Bigfoot to the cash register station and taps him on the shoulder. What the hell is he doing? The other Disciples seem unconcerned. Bigfoot turns and snarls, "You need somethin', faggot, or do you just got a death wish?"

Langdon smiles, reaches into the pocket of his jeans, comes out with a pearl-handled, double-barreled Derringer and pokes it into Bigfoot's big belly.

"Tell you what, you Neanderthal ape," Langdon says, somehow conveying menace in his soft Southern drawl. "What say I accompany you outside to make certain that unfortunate possibility does not occur."

I wonder if the sight of the Derringer or the word Neanderthal surprises the guy most. After a tense moment, the big man says, "Fuck it, ain't worth the bother." He turns back to the cashier, a red-haired teenage girl with braces on her teeth, pays his check and leaves, muttering something we can't hear. Of course, Bigfoot still could run over our cycles, but, for whatever reason, he doesn't.

Langdon slides the pistol back into his pocket as we join him at the cashier's station.

"Feed a cold, starve a fever, and confront a bully, my mama always said," he comments with a grin.

A man in his forties with a nametag on his shirt identifying him as Harlan, the Five Aces' manager, comes over to us.

"Your lunches are on me, boys. That guy was out of line. But if you're ever back this way, I highly recommend you sit in the civilians' dining area, not with the truckers."

NIGHT HAS fallen as the Devil's Disciples plus one roll into Savannah. As we bump along a brick-paved street through a residential neighborhood we come upon an older gent strolling purposefully along a sidewalk. He sports a neatly trimmed Vandyke and is nattily turned out in a white linen suit, Panama hat, and white buck shoes. He carries a battered brown leather briefcase, and taps the sidewalk on every stride with a brass-tipped walking stick.

I imagine this man and maybe his son as attorneys in practice together, the firm's name is something like Beauregard & Beauregard, PA, the name engraved on a shiny brass plaque bolted onto the front of an ivy-clad red brick row house. Maybe a bottle of Southern Comfort in the drawer of a scarred oak rolltop desk, to celebrate a courtroom victory, or a sunset. How much more genteel and satisfying (in my fantasy) than toiling in the billable-hour coal mine of Hartfield, Miller, Simon & Swenson, in that high-rise glass box in downtown Minneapolis. And in a family firm, you don't get fired.

The man glances at our passing motorcycle parade. He smiles and tips his hat. If the Disciples were a bona fide motorcycle gang, and began circling and taunting this elderly fellow like Lee Marvin and his band in *The Wild Ones*, he might produce a Derringer like Langdon's, or draw a sword embedded in the walking stick, and shoo them away.

Langdon has relatives in Savannah, he explained last night, an aunt and two cousins. The aunt, now in her eighties, is his father's sister, the cousins her sons. He has not seen or spoken with them in many years. His father made his money "from cotton and tobacco." Langdon is an only child. For some reason his parents never spoke about, a family feud developed, Langdon said.

"There were hints of infidelities, somebody slept with somebody they shouldn't have, and maybe of a joint business venture gone bad, I think I recall something about a sure-fire investment in a racehorse," he told me. "Sex and money! All very Southern Gothic. Think Tennessee Williams. Now I hear that Aunt Lucy is in failing health, and my cousins, Jubal and Nathan, who are named for Confederate generals, have failed in a number of business enterprises of their own, including a muffler shop franchise, a lumberyard, and a liquor store. How one could not make a go of a liquor store in Savannah is beyond me," Langdon told me. "I guess I'm getting soft, because I'm going to slip away while we're in Savannah, meet with the boys and do the right thing by the family, meaning that an appropriate amount of money will change hands." He smiled. "That being the only way family feuds ever do get resolved."

Langdon leads the group to a small white-frame house surrounded by a black wrought iron fence, located away from the fashionable neighborhoods and tourist attractions. Pots of red geraniums hang from the ceiling of the front porch. There is no sign and no other indication that this is anything but someone's residence. I wonder if Langdon has a friend in town who has invited us to dinner, although I wouldn't guess that friends of Langdon Lamont would live in a neighborhood such as this. Here, it might still be called "black bottom."

We follow Langdon into a parking lot covered with white gravel so deep that my rear wheel slides sideways and I almost dump the BMW.

"This is Mama Sally's," Langdon tells me. "Another regular stop for us. Only the locals know it. Aunt Lucy introduced me to it pre-estrangement. The best Southern cooking on the planet. An orgasmic experience, I tell you."

Dinner is served family-style at a large round oak table that is covered with platters and bowls filled with good Southern cooking. If nothing else, I'm certainly being well fed on this trip. I have a vision of me getting as big as Bigfoot. Maybe I'll go to Key West and sit on Slater Babcock until he talks.

The conversation over dinner is about anything but the sad history of the Tanner family, which I appreciate. Over dessert, Miles offers another of his quotations: "Happy families are all alike; every unhappy family is unhappy in its own way." He adds, "I'm feeling content and generous so I'll just tell you that's from . . ."

"Tolstoy's *Anna Karenina*!" Alan Dupree exclaims. "Had to read it in my comp lit class."

Miles looks annoyed just for a moment, then grins. "Okay, fair's fair, drinks are on me, retroactively."

Yes, I think, draining my coffee cup and pushing back from the table, as full as I think I've ever been, Tolstoy got that exactly right.

After dinner, we ride over to the Mansion on Forsyth Park, a grand old Colonial in the historic district. I dream that I am an infantry private—it is not clear in which army—in a bloody Civil War battle, and am relieved to awaken in the morning without injury.

By EIGHT A.M., we're on the road again, south on I-95 toward the Florida border and then through Jacksonville and the beachfront towns of the Palm Coast and into Daytona Beach. Langdon got up early and said he took care of his family business to everyone's satisfaction: "All will be forgiven, provided that my check clears," he joked.

It's unseasonably warm, the temperature in the high 70s, so it's tee shirts and jeans all around, except for Langdon, who's wearing a white aloha shirt with red flowers, and khaki shorts with his boots. I've been honored with the point position. Not long out of Savannah, we begin to encounter other groups of riders headed south, roaring past us over the speed limit, wolf pack after wolf pack of cycles streaking toward the biggest annual gathering of like-minded souls in the nation—Daytona Bike Week. They are mostly on Harleys, plus a smattering of other big-shouldered American brands like Indian and Buell and Victory, and custom jobs of unidentifiable make. Lowriders and ape bars and gleaming chrome and wild paint jobs no factory produced. These are genuine outlaws, the real deals. The women on the rear seats mostly are wearing leather halter tops and shorts, skimpy bikinis, or leathers.

I'm reminded of Hannah, my felonious Lolita. A few women ride their own bikes and look as though they could kick any man's ass if he suggested they should be relegated to a rear seat. All eyes front as they pass, not so much as a glance over at us; even though we wear the colors of an actual cycle gang, we reveal our true colors by cruising at the speed limit, which only pussies do.

The boys assured me they've never been hassled at Daytona for showing up on their Japanese bikes. In fact, a contingent of retirees from Boynton Beach showed up last year on Vespa motor scooters and was welcomed with amusement, never having to buy their own drinks in the beer tents, Langdon reported. The only real pariahs are those kids zooming around on "crotch rockets," those high-speed, low-slung racing bikes where you tuck yourself down beneath a streamlined cowling, chest on the gas tank, and gun it around town as if you're on the Daytona 500 race track, Tom explained. "Everyone hates those little shits," he said. "Me included."

The Daytona Beach exit coming up, Alan passes me and takes the lead. We follow him onto the exit ramp and swing east onto US Route 92 toward the Atlantic Ocean, bikers everywhere, ready to party hearty.

We begin to pass municipal light posts festooned with banners reading "DAYTONA BEACH/WELCOME BIKERS." The city is delighted to have the revenue Bike Week generates, Tom told me, but the residents would probably like it better if it came from a convention of free-spending Baptists or Knights of Columbus.

We swing off 92 and navigate along side streets through downtown Daytona Beach, which are impossibly congested with Bike Week traffic, then head over the Main Street causeway across the Halifax River and onto a long, narrow barrier island. We follow Alan left onto South Atlantic Avenue and come to the community of Seabreeze, identified by a grey wooden sign with white lettering and a carved seagull.

Alan leads us into the driveway of a two-story white house built on stilts so that the first floor is a good eight feet above sea level. We kill the engines, lean our cycles onto their kickstands and dismount, stretching stiff backs, rotating necks, unbuckling helmets as the hot engines tick.

"We always rent this beach house," Victor says. "Eight hundred a night during Bike Week, but it beats the hell out of motels, where the other guests are up all night shouting and fighting, or camping out on the beach, which gets even louder and funkier, and the mosquitoes bite like piranhas."

"Pricey, but not so bad divided by six," Harold adds.

"By seven," I say.

"*The Magnificent Seven*," says Alan, who is more into classic movies than classic literature, as he laughs and slaps me on the back.

It was lunchtime when we arrived, so we unpacked, then rode to a waterfront seafood shack they liked for lobster rolls and iced sweet tea. After that, Alan led us on a sightseeing cruise around town, for my benefit. We took a stroll on the beach, then went back to the house, had cold beers on the deck, and chatted about politics, and the upcoming base-ball season, and how good it was that home prices were rebounding—just guys, shooting the breeze. It was nice; I almost felt like my old, pre-family-tragedy self again.

That night, as is the custom, Miles cooks steaks for dinner on a gas grill on the deck, which we eat with a salad Vic pre-pares, and several bottles of good cabernet sauvignon. Dessert is a key lime pie. It is Harold's job to e-mail a list of provisions to the rental agent that will be waiting for us upon arrival.

After dinner, we stay up late drinking Ramos Gin Fizzes, "a true Southern gentlemen's drink," Langdon announces, which I watch him prepare in the kitchen while the others relax out-side on the deck.

Langdon learned the drink recipe during "a lost decade" in New Orleans, he tells me. Ramos Gin Fizzes are not stan-dard cocktail fare in Minnesota. Langdon, whistling "Swan-nee River," blends gin, lemon juice, egg whites, sugar, cream, orange flower water and soda water in a cocktail shaker. He pours the creamy, frothy concoction into tall chilled Tom Col-lins glasses and carries them outside on a big plastic tray. We enjoy our drinks as an electric bug catcher announces its kills with crackling zaps. Langdon makes several trips back into the kitchen to fix more gin fizzes. I lose count of how many I drink; they go down easy, like milk shakes.

During a pause in the conversation, Vic says, "Why don't you offer a belated toast, Jack, even though we're already in our cups."

On the spot, all I can come up with is: " 'No deduction otherwise allowable under this chapter shall be allowed for any item . . . With respect to an activity which is of a type generally considered to constitute entertainment, amusement, or recreation, unless the taxpayer establishes that the item was directly related to, or, in the case an item directly preceding or following a substantial and bona fide business discussion . . .' "

Silence.

Then Tom, the Harvard Business School professor, grins and says, "The tax attorney quotes the United States tax code!"

"I bet he can cite chapter and verse," Vic says.

Everyone looks at me expectantly. I instantly regret this nerdy, show-offy slip, it's the gin fizzes talking, I'd like to think, and not the real me coming out, but I admit the clause is from "Title 26, Subtitle A, Chapter 1, Subchapter B, Part IX, Section 274."

"Here, here," Langdon says, raising his glass. "He's telling us that this trip is not deductible. Very useful info!"

At three A.M., we call it quits and turn in. I can't remember the last time I've been this tipsy; passing out and falling asleep is a distinction without a difference.

14

I wake up at seven A.M. to the aroma of bacon frying, which reminds me of boyhood Saturday mornings when my father took over breakfast duties. Dad was a marketing executive with 3M in Saint Paul, mom taught history at Saint Thomas Academy, which I attended, and I was their only child. We lived in the Highland Park neighborhood, which is very much like Edina.

Dad's standing Saturday menu was blueberry pancakes with melted butter and heated syrup—one of my cakes always formed into the letter "J"—plus thick-cut smoked bacon, freshly squeezed OJ, and creamy whole milk, none of that thin, fat-free, 1-, or 2-percent stuff of today. The syrup came in a metal can the shape of a little log cabin. These cabins were rinsed and lined up on a shelf in my bedroom; I must have had a north woods village of thirty of them by the time I graduated from high school and left for college.

I HADN'T thought about any of that for decades. So far this ride to Key West seems more a trip down memory lane than a transformation of any kind. I'm still good old Jack Tanner, as far as I can tell. Perhaps the most effective thing I can do to Slater Babcock is to turn him in to the IRS—in my experience, every taxpayer has something to hide—or hit him with a briefcase, as Pete Dye suggested. Of course, my briefcase is at home, but I understood what Pete meant by that: I'm a lawyer, not a fighter.

I swing my feet onto the floor, feeling a bit dizzy. I pull on a tee shirt and jeans and go to the kitchen. There I find Vic, shirtless and shoeless, wearing boxer shorts, a Red Sox cap, and a chef's apron, making waffles, bacon, and link sausages.

"Wow," I say. "Is this a beach house or a cruise ship?"

"Welcome aboard the SS Purcell!" he says. "I can offer you coffee or espresso, regular or unleaded."

I perch on a stool at the center island.

"A cappuccino would be great, but I'll make it," I tell him. A fancy espresso machine sits on the counter near the juicer. It's got more controls than my motorcycle.

"Let me do it. You could hurt yourself with that thing."

Soon the whole gang is gathered around the kitchen table, feasting on Vic's spread and chatting happily like kids in the dining hall at summer camp.

"So what's today's agenda?" I ask.

Alan explains, "We always start with a ride up and down International Speedway Boulevard through the city. Then we head over to the beach and take a stroll for a little exercise."

"Exercise being defined as ogling the topless babes," adds Miles.

"The trick being to savor the view without getting stomped by their boyfriends," says Tom.

"Sounds like a plan," I tell them.

Langdon pushes back from the table.

"Dinner is at a seafood place we like a short ride up the coast in Ormond Beach. Basically one does not want to be in downtown Daytona after dark. That's when the vampires come out, if you catch my drift."

I do.

"How bad does it get?"

"The great majority of Bike Week attendees are well-behaved," Harold answers. "But there are some who come looking for trouble and find it. Often they're not the bikers. You get your survivalists, rednecks, gangbangers, and Florida crackers who don't like outsiders taking over their town. And everyone's armed. Florida's gun laws are pretty much the same as Dodge City's in the days of Wyatt Earp. They'd just laugh at Langdon and his little pistol. These fuckers are armed like a SEAL team. Best for the likes of us to steer clear."

"Law enforcement does a good job, but they can't be everywhere all the time," Vic adds. "There were three shootings last year, one a fatality, all after midnight. And some years ago, we heard, a guy ran his Ford F-150 right into a crowd on a sidewalk. Killed three people before the truck hit a building, or something. The crowd dragged him out and stomped him to death. Although that might be an apocryphal story."

It's sunny and hot, no wind off the ocean to mitigate the humidity. We're strolling the beach, shirtless, the others in shorts or bathing suits; all I have are my jeans. I'm feeling relaxed. Earlier, Victor Purcell and I had coffee out on the deck of the beach house while the others were in the kitchen.

"I lost a son," Vic said.

"I'm sorry," I told him.

"The summer before Brian's senior year in high school, he was staying at a friend's house on Cape Cod, in Wellfleet. It was late August. Football practice had started. Brian was a wide receiver. He was much more than that, but that's what he was in football. The other boys with him were teammates. Some of them were swimming, not far offshore. Brian was on the beach, tossing a football. There was a rip current. One of the boys, Jerry Docherty, was caught in it and started yelling for help. He apparently didn't know you had to swim parallel to the beach to get out of it instead of heading directly in. Brian, who was a good swimmer, went out to get Jerry. I guess he panicked, and grabbed onto Brian. They both drowned."

The only thing I can think to say is, "Do you have other children, Vic?" I regret this instantly, as if having another child can somehow mitigate his loss.

"Yes," he answers. "We are blessed with another son, Matt, who is an architect, and he works with me designing our shopping malls; and a daughter, Gina, who is an investment banker in New York."

"That's a blessing," I said, and we finished our coffee in silence.

A MODERATE wind has come up and is raising whitecaps on the water, good enough for the surfers and Boogie Boarders. I think about young Brian Purcell. One thing about being consumed by your own troubles is you can forget that others may be hurting, too.

And then, all of a sudden, there she is, Hannah the felonious hitchhiker, wading out of the surf, topless, bikinibottomed, then strolling toward a group of men and women, obviously a hardcore biker crowd, set up with coolers over by one of the lifeguard stations. Some are boisterously watching a beach volleyball game, others are just grab-assing around; all are drinking from plastic cups and beer bottles.

I stop. My companions keep walking down the beach. I move closer and see it's not Hannah, it's another girl who could be her sister. One of her nipples and her navel are pierced.

One of the bikers in the group walks my way. He is tall, shirtless, with the carved physique of a serious weightlifter.

"Like what you see, amigo?" he says. He must have noticed me staring at that girl. "That's Linda, and she's for rent. Five hundred for a half day, twelve hundred and she'll stay the night."

Smiling as he says it. Just two guys discussing a business transaction.

"Thanks," I answer, "but I have other commitments."

The man shrugs and heads back toward his group. "Well, whatever floats your boat, dude."

Thanks but I have other commitments? How lame is that? What a big bad biker dude I've turned out to be.

At seven p.m. we are at the Green Dolphin Inn, the roadhouse Langdon mentioned. There appear to be no outlaw bikers in the place, which is precisely why the Disciples make this one of their regular stops. We're seated in a booth having beers and studying the menu when a woman comes hurrying through the entrance door and asks the bartender, "Who owns the cycles out in the lot?"

"They're ours," Harold says.

"Well there's a monster truck rollin' right over the whole lot of 'em. Someone should call 911."

As someone does, we hurry outside, along with a number of other patrons. A big black pickup truck with a raised chassis and huge tires is plowing back and forth over our motorcycles as the Steppenwolf song "Born To Be Wild" booms from the truck's sound system.

"Christ, it's that idiot from the truck stop Langdon faced down," Alan says. "He must've recognized our bikes, or come in the bar and spotted us."

Langdon pulls out his Derringer and fires two rounds into one of the truck's tires, but the little .32 caliber slugs just bounce off. Hearing the gunshots, Bigfoot grins, hits the brakes, and points a long-barrel revolver out of the driver's side window.

"Gun!" Miles shouts.

Everyone scatters, some running back into the bar, others, including me, taking cover behind cars, as Bigfoot begins firing off rounds, not seeming to actually aim at anyone, then guns it out of the parking lot, tires spewing gravel, and roars off down US Route 1.

Minutes later, two Volusia County Sheriff's cruisers, lights and sirens, come barreling down the highway from the other direction and squeal into the parking lot. Four deputies slide out and crouch behind the doors, guns drawn. Seeing only the wrecked cycles and people hiding behind cars, one of the deputies reaches into the cruiser, pulls out a microphone and says over the cruiser's PA system:

"Everyone face down on the ground, arms stretched out front!"

A moment of confusion, no one moving.

The deputy's amplified voice shouts again: "On the ground now! Grab the gravel!"

Only when all of us are lying on the ground as ordered do the deputies ease out from behind the car doors.

"Nobody move till I say," another of the deputies orders. He walks over to a man in his twenties and says, "We got a call about a truck running over motorcycles, and then another call about shots fired. First thing is, who was doing the shooting?"

"The guy in the truck," the young man answers. "He drove off just before you arrived."

The deputy moves over to Langdon.

"That right, sir?"

Langdon starts to turn over as he answers; the deputy puts his boot hard on Langdon's back, pushing him back down. So much for the "sir."

"Didn't say turn over. I asked if that's what happened."

"Yes," Langdon answers. "We saw the guy a few days ago at a truck stop in Virginia. We didn't get along all that well."

As this deputy has been asking questions, the others have been moving from person to person, patting them down. One by one they all say, "Clear." No guns. Langdon has thrown his Derringer into a trashcan, where the deputies don't look. Later, he will recover it.

"Okay, y'all can stand up," a deputy wearing sergeant's stripes says.

As we get to our feet, Harold asks, "Where's Tom?"

"Somebody missing?" the sergeant asks.

"Got a man down!" one of the other deputies calls out.

I look over and see Tom Jarvis, the Harvard professor, lying motionless on the gravel, with crimson blood pooling beneath his head.

THE NEXT morning we're in the beach house kitchen, seated around the breakfast table. We are the Magnificent Six now. Tom is dead. A bullet ricocheting off something hit him in the left temple. Someone got the license number of the truck. Calvin T. Laloosh, aka Bigfoot, is now in the Volusia County jail, charged with murder in the first degree, which any competent defense attorney should be able to deal down to second degree, intent being hard to prove when you're high on alcohol and dexies and apparently not aiming at anyone.

Laloosh has been in trouble before, Harold learned from the sheriff's department, with assault convictions and firearms violations on his rap sheet. He did a three-year stretch in Raiford, the prison, Harold was told, where the state's death chamber is located, offering the condemned a choice of lethal injection or electrocution—a choice Laloosh may now have to make, depending upon the skill of his lawyer. He is employed by a coast-to-coast moving company, and lives alone in a trailer park in Deltona.

He was arrested in his trailer without resistance. The SWAT Team found his pistol in his pit bull's doghouse behind the trailer. The dog is now in the care of the Volusia County humane society. The duty sergeant, sympathetic, told Harold all this.

None of us slept last night. We were at the sheriff's headquarters until midnight, giving statements, along with the other bar patrons who witnessed the event. Then Harold went to the county coroner's office to identify Tom's body. Afterward, he called Kathy Jarvis in Cambridge to break the tragic news. She is flying to Daytona Beach later this morning, and their two sons are flying in separately in the afternoon.

Vic has made scrambled eggs and toast but no one is very hungry. We're drinking coffee and dividing up the necessary tasks.

"So it's agreed," Miles says, checking the yellow legal pad on which he's been taking notes. "I'll coordinate with the funeral home in Cambridge on transportation and arrangements. Harold, you've got the family, Kathy and the boys, arriving at the airport at various times today. Alan is booking us on Tom's flight back to Boston. Vic is handling any follow-up with the sheriff's department. Langdon will stay in touch with the Volusia County district attorney's office about testifying at the trial."

"I can see about the cycles," I offer.

"Probably nothing there to salvage, but the insurance adjusters will want a look," Vic says.

I tell them I'll arrange to have the cycles taken to an auto or motorcycle repair shop and give everyone the address for their insurance people.

Everyone falls silent, left to our own thoughts about what has happened to our friend. I envision a "missing man" formation, as pilots do for a lost comrade, if these men ever ride together again.

THE FOLLOWING morning I'm standing at a car rental counter at the Daytona Beach International Airport, wearing a golf shirt, khaki slacks, and running shoes, my cycle rider attire stowed in my saddlebags. I am a motorcycle man no more.

I'm with Harold Whittaker, who is signing papers for a silver Taurus. The car is for me, but I can't rent it because I don't have a driver's license. It was in my wallet, which Hannah took.

Harold and I go out to the lot, get into the Taurus, Harold driving. He shows the rental papers to the attendant, and drives down the street to where he is parked. He gives me a hug and says, "God speed and keep you safe Jack. You're a good man. Call me when you get back home."

He'd given me his business card back at the beach house, as had Alan Dupree, Miles Standish, Langdon Lamont, and Vic Purcell. They wished me luck and apologized for being unable to stay with me on the rest of my journey, but with Tom Jarvis dead, they're needed back home. And at some point they'll have to come back here for Calvin Laloosh's trial, unless there's some sort of plea bargain. I feel that I've become as close to these men in our brief time together as any other friends I have, like soldiers who've been through combat together. We've promised to stay in touch. Maybe we will.

When I was packing my saddlebags, I found Langdon's Derringer tucked in it. I thought about returning it, then put it back. I understood that Langdon meant this as a gift from one friend to another, without thinking that the Jack Tanner he'd come to know would shoot anyone with it, except possibly in self-defense.

15

As I approach the entrance ramp to I-95 heading south out of Daytona Beach, I notice a girl wearing a backpack, hitchhiking. She's holding a cardboard sign reading "Key West," and turns it toward me, raising her eyebrows in expectation. She is pretty, with her brown hair twisted into braids, in her late teens or early twenties, wearing jeans and a University of Florida "Go Gators!" tee shirt that exposes her belly.

Yeah, right. Fool me once . . .

Maybe she really is a college girl, like Hope, whom I should rescue from the possibility that a serial killer will be driving the next car that comes along. Or maybe the Gators tee shirt is a ruse, and she is another highway predator, like Hannah. Harold didn't opt for the extra car rental insurance. Does the basic package cover theft by renter stupidity? By honey trap?

I nod and smile as I pass her by. No hard feelings. Sorry, sweetie, but I have my reasons. I see in the rearview mirror that she's giving me the finger.

I accelerate onto the highway, running up to eighty before I check the speedometer, then ease back down to seventy. This rental car has GPS and satellite radio. I find the Beach Boys singing "409." Nostalgic and nice. I was good at school, I had the school thing down pat, the academics, sports, and the social life, all through high school, college, and law school. Too bad a person can't remain a student forever. It's what happens after graduation that can be so very problematic.

Four hours down I-95 I impulsively swing onto Exit 2D toward Miami Beach. I've been there on several family

~ 111 ~

vacations and an occasional business trip. I'm feeling exhausted, even after a relatively short drive in a comfortable car. No wonder, given all that's happened, and the uncertainty about what might happen next.

I'll check into the Loews, one of the nice oceanfront hotels on Collins Avenue, and use it as a staging area before driving on to Key West—or as a rest stop before catching a flight home. Whichever seems right at the time. I've begun to understand what it means to go with the flow, as they said in the sixties. I feel that I'm pretty much drifting now, as if floating in the Gulf Stream, headed to wherever the current takes me, as if someone or something else is in charge of my fate, which is a relief, because I've not been doing so great at being in charge of myself.

It's early afternoon, sunny, and seventy-eight degrees according to the digital thermometer readout on the dashboard instrument panel, with a cloudless azure sky. I cross the MacArthur Causeway onto the island city of Miami Beach. Huge cruise ships are moored in line on a long pier to my right, their stacked decks rising up from the hulls like layers on a tall cake.

Jenna and I once took one of these ships on a Caribbean cruise, stopping at Barbados, Saint Lucia, Antigua, and Saint Kitts, to celebrate our tenth anniversary. The ports-of-call were nice, but Jenna got seasick in some heavy weather during the return voyage. I thought the ship rather tacky, like a floating Vegas casino with shuffleboard and programmed activities: "The mah-jongg tournament starts on the Lido Deck in fifteen minutes! Mah-jongg in fifteen!" We decided our vacations would be landlocked from then on.

At the end of the causeway I go left onto Ocean Drive, enjoying the retro angular pastel architecture of the Art Deco District in South Beach, heading north into Miami Beach proper. There, it's less young, funky, and Latino than the SoBe neighborhood; I feel more at home, and can speak the language, having forgotten all of my high school Spanish.

The Loews Miami Beach was the site of an NATP (National Association of Tax Professionals) convention that I attended six years ago. Wives were invited, but Jenna had to stay home to play in a tennis tournament at our club.

Section 179 of the Internal Revenue Code allows a 50 percent deduction for convention-related expenses, a happy fact that accounted for the selection of ocean-view, instead of city view, rooms at the Loews, and steak instead of chicken on the banquet menu, none of which was attractive enough to entice Jenna to skip her tournament.

I swing into the hotel's circular drive and park in front of the entrance. A young valet, wearing a white tunic with brass buttons, opens the car door and greets me with a cheery, "Welcome to the Loews, sir!" If the bellman thinks it odd that my only luggage is black leather motorcycle saddlebags, he doesn't show it as he lifts them out of the trunk. Even though it's still high season, the hotel has a room for me, I find, because of a cancellation.

OF COURSE, I hadn't packed a bathing suit for this trip. Who knew I'd be lounging by a pool in Miami Beach, an unintentional tourist? So I buy one in one of the lobby shops, flowered Hawaiian-style boxer trunks. Not my style, but all they have in my size, at the rip-off, captive-audience price of fifty-five dollars. I change in my room, and feel self-conscious as I parade through the ornate lobby on the way to the pool, wearing the trunks, along with a tee shirt, and rubber flip-flops, which I also bought at the shop.

Poolside, there are older men and women who shouldn't wear swimsuits; snowmobile suits would be more flattering, covering up their protruding potbellies, skinny, hairy legs, floppy boobs, big cabooses, and varicose veins, all held together with the chalky white skin of new arrivals from the north. Here and there are younger women with knockout bodies displayed in tiny bikinis not much wider than dental floss that would cause a scandal back home at the Edina Country Club pool, at least among the women members.

The pool area includes a village of canvas cabanas, an outdoor restaurant and tiki bar, and row upon row of reclining beach chairs around a pool big enough to be a small lake. The Atlantic, with a wide sandy beach, is right there beyond a low metal security fence with a locking gate that opens with your room card—no riffraff beachcombers need apply.

A pretty young woman with short blonde hair, in white shorts and a white form-fitting Loews tee shirt, which highlights her bronze suntan, appears, toting two thick white terry-cloth towels.

"Hi, I'm Julie," she chirps. "Would you like a lounge chair, or poolside cabana, or maybe a cabana out on the beach?"

"Just a chair by the pool would be fine," I tell her.

Bending over in those tight little uniform shorts—how could you not give her a big tip?—Julie places one of the towels over a chair and rolls the other into a pillow.

"I can get you a drink or a lunch menu," she says. "And maybe you'd like a massage appointment?"

I follow her gaze over to a series of canvas tents across a lawn set up for croquet; the tents contain massage tables, two of them in use. No thanks, I tell her. I order an iced tea and lie back on the chair with my arms behind my head, taking in the scene. I'm feeling more like a tourist than an avenging angel.

After a swim and a poolside sandwich, I go back to my room, change, and retrieve my car, then cruise up and down Collins Avenue, seeing the sights: the resort hotels, condo buildings, marinas with fleets of motor yachts and sailboats, and the Bal Harbour Shops where Jenna liked to shop when we stayed at the Loews for three days after that cruise. Nothing here I want to see, really. Just killing time, avoidance behavior, now that I'm within striking distance of Key West, which I've come to think of as Hadleyville, the town where Gary Cooper faced down the bad guys in *High Noon*, one of my all-time favorite movies.

"COME HERE often?"

A woman seated one stool away is talking to me. She looks good for a woman her age, which is, what? In this time of plastic surgery, Botox, dental bleaching and bonding, power Pilates and Hatha yoga, personal trainers, vegan/good carb/ low fat/juice diets, spray tans and lip augmentation, who can tell anymore? She has short brown hair and is wearing sunglasses, a tight white V-neck tee shirt with gold-glitter lettering saying "Cannes Film Festival 2008," gold lamé capri pants on her long legs, and red slingback pumps.

"No, I don't," I answer.

She smiles and slides over onto the stool beside me and we chat. Her name is Samantha, no last name given (yellow warning light: Hannah didn't give her last name either). She is originally from Seattle, graduated from the University of Washington with a degree in psychology, worked at "this job and that," and now "travels."

I tell her my background, up to a point. She asks why I'm in Miami Beach, and I say I'm here on business.

"Me too," she says with a smile and a wink, and then shocks me by telling me that she advertises her "escort services" on adult websites, and is having a glass of pinot noir before keeping an appointment for a "sensual massage" for a fee of "two hundred roses an hour" with "a client" staying here at the hotel.

I'm tempted to ask her why an educated, beautiful woman is in her line of work, debating whether this would be, what? Sexist? Offensive? Who am I to judge anyone?

There's a chiming sound in her purse. She takes out a cell phone, scans a text message, checks her watch, slides off the stool, gives me an air kiss and says, "Ciao, Jack. You're nice."

"Thanks, you too."

Samantha doesn't know it, but to me, "nice" at this point is not a compliment, it is a statement of my failure to evolve into someone like Hank Whitby, my take-no-prisoners neighbor. This good old nice Jack might as well just head back home.

She takes a business card from her purse and puts it on the bar. It's made of creamy, thick stock, and has embossed black lettering, a fancy law-firm quality card. On it is just a phone number with a Miami area code. Classy, like Samantha herself.

"Now don't write this number on a men's room wall, Jack," she says. "If you stay here awhile and want some company, call me."

She departs. I pay my tab and decide to find a restaurant for dinner, leaving her card on the bar for a better prospect than me. I amuse myself by imagining that Samantha is an undercover vice cop, out to entrap johns and put their names in the newspaper. Actually, that happened to one of my law firm's clients once, generating a few extra billable hours.

THE MOON is a gray silver above a calm dark sea as I stroll the beach after a dinner at Yucatan, a very good Cuban restaurant in South Beach, which the hotel concierge recommended. I enjoyed the meal, but it's no fun dining alone at such a nice place. Jenna would have liked it.

I pause, looking up at the starry nighttime sky. I was a junior astronomer as a young boy, getting an expensive Galileo telescope for my ninth birthday. I memorized all the phases of the moon, waning and waxing, full, gibbous, and crescent, and the constellations visible in the northern hemisphere, Leo, Virgo, Gemini, Orion . . .

That's a crescent moon up there. But those constellations? Not a clue, nothing that looks like a lion or a hunter or a maiden, or any other recognizable connect-the-dots shape. Someone, I can't recall who, told me your brain is like a computer hard drive. You have room for a finite amount of data storage, and when your memory bank is full, and you learn something new, some old fact gets deleted. The tax code must have wiped out my memory of astronomy.

I'm startled by a voice behind me.

"Beautiful, isn't it? The nighttime sky over the water."

I turn to see a woman standing there, my second chance meeting with a female today. She points heavenward. "There's Cassiopeia, Ursa Major and Minor, and Hydra." She smiles. "I'm forgetting my manners." She offers her hand, which I take. "Vickie Blatchford. Sorry for sneaking up on you like that."

She speaks with the British upper-class accent called "Oxbridge." Illuminated by the moonlight, she looks about my age. She is barefoot, and has shoulder-length auburn hair, green eyes, and a slender body under a blue-and-white striped boating shirt, and white shorts.

"Hi. Jack Tanner. Are you staying at the Loews?" We're just outside the hotel's beach gate.

"No, I'm staying on a boat, actually."

I look out over the water. A very large motor yacht, lights ablaze, is anchored maybe a quarter-mile offshore.

"Oh, not that one," Vickie laughs. "Mine is just a little sailboat, moored at a yacht club near Fisher Island. I caught a bite to eat at a nice Cuban bistro near here and decided to have a walk as a digestif."

"It wasn't Yucatan, was it?"

"Why yes, that's the place."

"I ate there tonight, too."

Vickie invites me to see her boat. On an impulse, I accept her invitation. Going with the flow. We ride over to the Admiral Yacht Club on her rented Honda motor scooter, Vickie at the helm, me again a passenger on a two-wheeler.

WE'RE SEATED on a padded bench in the cockpit of her boat, sipping gin and tonic. Her "little sailboat" is a thirty-seven-foot Endeavour sloop, black-hulled with a red stripe, named *Sea Sprite*, which she intends to sail to the Turks and Caicos

Islands, with whatever island ports of call seem appealing along the way, she told me when we arrived and boarded.

"My husband Nigel and I planned this voyage for three years," she says. "He's in politics. Always difficult for him to get away for an extended period. We decided to finally just do it."

Does she know she just quoted a Nike advertising slogan? Nigel Blatchford. The name sounds familiar. Sir Nigel, the business tycoon turned cabinet minister?

Vickie sips her G&T and pushes her hair back behind her ears, a charming, unconscious gesture, intensely feminine.

"*Was* in politics, I should say. Nigel died five months ago, of a stroke. I can't get used to the past tense."

"I don't think you ever do get used to it."

"We chartered this boat and paid in advance," she continues. "Under the circumstances, getting the money back would have been no problem. But, against the advice of friends and family, I decided to make the trip by myself. I suppose I thought it might make me feel close to him. I've sailed all my life, never as a captain, but I think I've picked up enough to handle the boat alone."

The wind has picked up, and a British flag, which Vickie brought with her, is snapping on its stern staff.

"Let's go below," she says. "We wouldn't want our drinks to blow away."

The main cabin is all brass and mahogany, with a teak parquet deck. Vickie queues up Bach on the stereo system and refreshes our drinks in the galley. I recognize that the selection is the Glenn Gould recording of Bach's *The Goldberg Variations* because Jenna, who loves classical music, gave me that CD one year for my birthday. She did that sometimes, giving me things that she wanted. One year I told her I was giving her a golf trip for two to Scotland, even though she doesn't play golf, but I didn't follow through, which is also one problem with my golf swing. I don't show off for Vickie by naming the tune. If she asked me any other question about classical music, I'd have to abandon ship.

After several more drinks, the wind still howling outside, with the music and dim lights from copper lanterns, and the warmth of the gin in my bloodstream, I feel content.

Vickie slides closer on the bench seat, and touches my arm.

"Do you mind if I ask why you're here, in Miami Beach, unaccompanied? I don't mean to pry."

She grins, wrinkling her nose.

"But I will ask anyway."

And for the third time since leaving home, I blurt out my story. When I'm finished, Vickie says, "I'd very much like you to spend the night, Jack, if you want. I think we both could use some company before we go our separate ways. It's possible neither one of us will survive our journeys."

This said matter-of-factly, as if the stars will determine our fates and we are mere spectators. Which I now believe, too.

We spend the night together in the stateroom's comfortable round bed, cozy under a goose down quilt with the air conditioner on, me in my boxers, Vickie in a tee shirt and panties, hugging for a moment, then her chaste kiss on my cheek, and finding our own positions in the bed like an old married couple, back to back, pretending, maybe, that the other person is our absent spouse.

IN THE morning, Vickie makes coffee in a cold press, strong and good, apparently assuming, correctly, that that's what an American wants, and tea for herself, with some croissants and orange marmalade she has in a well-provisioned galley. Then we ride to the Loews on her scooter, and wave good-bye as she putts off down Collins Avenue.

I shower and check out of the hotel at ten A.M., get a map of the Keys from the concierge, and embark upon the last leg

of my long journey. By now I've given up on the idea of for-
mulating some sort of plan before I arrive, or of being someone
else when I do. I recall the Woody Allen dictum that "showing
up is 80 percent of life." I'll just have to show up and improvise the remaining 20 percent.

16

I've driven along some scenic roadways before, including the Great River Road in Minnesota running along the bank of the Mississippi, US Route 20 through Yellowstone in Wyoming, the Pacific Coast Highway in Northern California, and, with college friends during one spring break, a wild ride in a Ford panel van with a psychedelic paint job on Mexico's Federal Highway 1 from Tijuana all the way to Cabo San Lucas. But none is prettier than US Route 1 connecting the Florida mainland with Key West, island hopping on one hundred miles of bridges and causeways, with the calm blue Gulf of Mexico to the west and frothy white-capped Atlantic Ocean to the east.

After a day in Miami Beach, it's time to begin the endgame of my quixotic expedition. I left Edina on a Harley Road King, hitched a ride on Harold's Honda, bought a BMW touring bike, and now will roll into Key West in a rented Ford Taurus. Not exactly a triumphant arrival, but the best I can do under the circumstances.

I wonder if Vickie Blatchford has set sail, hoping to reconnect with the ghost of Sir Nigel somewhere out there in the deep blue Caribbean Sea. Is it possible she has planned a suicide voyage? Might she scuttle the boat and sink down beneath the waves, thinking that their spirits might reconnect for eternity? I hope not. She is such a beautiful, intelligent and charming woman. But I know how grief can change a person.

After two hours, I enter the Village of Islamorada, located at Mile Marker 82, which is how locations are designated along the Overseas Highway, as this stretch of US Route 1 is called. The Loews concierge told me about the mile markers, which measure the one hundred fifty-six mile distance between Miami and Key West.

Islamorada is a world-famous fishing village, I know, because a group of my Edina golfing buddies once organized a fishing trip here. It was during a week in April, income tax season for my clients, so I couldn't join them. They came back with sunburns and photos showing tarpon, sailfish and tuna they'd caught and released. I regretted missing the trip. I've done a lot of lake fishing in Minnesota, catching walleye, northern pike, bass, and a few of the elusive muskies. But I've never gone after the really big boys you needed a fighting chair to boat. That would have been an interesting experience.

I stop for gas at a 7-Eleven, go inside, and ask the young girl behind the counter about a place to get a sandwich. She's tanned, thin, and pretty, with short blonde hair and azure eyes, and is wearing a white halter top, black jogging shorts and flip-flops. She has a little blue-green dolphin tattooed just above her left hip.

"Good sandwich?" she says, crinkling her nose. "Well, mister, we've got hot dogs that've been turning on those rollers for a couple of days, and some sandwiches in that cooler, tuna, chicken salad, egg salad, hoagies . . . One of my jobs is to keep changing the sell-by dates on the sandwiches."

She smiles.

"So I'd say, definitely not here. But just down the road, at Mile Marker 79.9, there's a marina, the Blue Marlin, that's got okay fried clam rolls and stuff."

"Thanks for that," I say, and stuff two dollars into the tip jar on the counter.

I PARK the Taurus in a sandy lot behind a rambling, two-story, white wooden building with peeling paint, slatted green hurricane shutters, and a rusted tin roof. The Blue Marlin Marina has obviously been around a long time and survived many a tropical storm.

I walk around to the front, where charter fishing boats are lined up along three long L-shaped docks jutting out into the waters of Florida Bay, waiting for their afternoon runs. There had been good fishing that morning, as evidenced by crewmen cleaning fish at stations along the docks, with pelicans and seagulls swooping down as the fish cleaners toss innards into the water.

A bald, portly, sunburned, middle-aged man in a Hawaiian shirt, canvas shorts, and boat shoes is having his picture taken standing beside a tall hoist which holds a very large fish suspended head down by its tail. A blue marlin, I think. Such a noble and beautiful animal. It should have been freed to return to the Gulf Stream, not strung up like this and then stuffed and mounted, to hang on some rec room wall in Iowa or Indiana or wherever. I have the urge to go over to the hoist, lower the fish to the dock, and give the man a lecture on the sanctity of life, including the life of this fish. I think again of horses killed on Civil War battlefields.

But that would be pointless. Instead, I go into the marina building in search of a sandwich and a beer. Inside the door is a store that sells bait, tackle, marine equipment, nautical clothing, and groceries. One wall is covered with the photos of people who've been here to fish; some are posed outside with their trophies hanging from that same hoist, others are strapped into fighting chairs on the decks of boats, their poles bent under the weight of whatever they've hooked. Many of the photos are very old, in faded black and white, others are in color. Included in the gallery are shots of famous people such as Ernest Hemingway, Ted Williams, Joe DiMaggio with Marilyn Monroe, John Wayne, Clint Eastwood, and Bill Clinton with a woman who is not Hillary, all posing with their catches. A veritable Islamorada Fishing Hall of Fame.

"Help you?" a man behind the bait counter asks as I'm studying the photos. He looks old enough to have sold bait to

Hemingway back in the 1930s. He is wearing a tee shirt bearing the marina's name, and tan canvas shorts with stains on them, probably fish blood.

"Are you serving lunch?" I ask.

The man nods toward a doorway in the back wall.

"Right through there," he says, then picks up a little net and begins scooping up minnows floating belly up in a tank. Maybe they're going on the lunch menu.

The door opens into a large pine-paneled room with three big fans with woven bamboo blades slowly turning on the ceiling. The tables are filled with customers, many of them looking windblown and tanned as if they'd been out on the charter boats that morning. More trophy fish are mounted on the walls, along with the heads of wild game: a bighorn sheep, a boar with long ivory tusks, an elk with a big rack of antlers, a black bear with an eternal snarl displaying pointed yellow teeth, and a moose. A sad graveyard.

I find the one empty table and sit. A waitress comes over, hands me a menu, and says, "Specials today are conch chowder, lobster mac and cheese, a grouper sandwich, breaded and fried or blackened, and baked mahi mahi."

I order a draft Red Stripe and a blackened grouper sandwich. As I'm eating, the waitress comes over and asks, "Would you mind a little company?" I look over to see a man and woman and a young girl standing just inside the dining room doorway, looking my way.

"No, that'd be fine," I tell her.

The family comes over and takes chairs. "Appreciate it," the man says. "I'm Larry Blaisdell. This is my wife, Marla, and our daughter, Lucy."

I stand up and shake his hand. "Jack Tanner. No problem at all."

I learn that they are from Toronto. I can hear that Canadian "oot" and "aboot" in their speech. They are driving to Key West, just like me. Lucy is twelve and on spring break.

I'm reminded of my own family on vacation. Long live happy families.

Today is Hope's twenty-first birthday. A hard day for me, and for Jenna, too, back at The Sanctuary, if she's still as lucid as she was during my visit, and remembers. I can recall all of Hope's birthdays, but now think about her ninth. A week before it, Jenna asked Hope what she wanted. "I want to be ten," she said, in all seriousness. Children always want to be older, adults want to be younger.

Now Hope would never be older than nineteen. She would never graduate from college, or go to Europe and maybe meet her future husband there, as Jenna did, or have a family of her own, or a career . . . or do whatever else she wanted. I thought about calling Jenna this morning, but decided not to. The call would have been too painful for us both.

Larry has been saying something to me, I realize.

". . . and so the hotel clerk apologized and upgraded us to a suite at no extra cost."

We chat for the rest of the lunch. A nice family.

"All happy families are alike . . ."

17

I cross the causeway onto the island of Key West. I've finally arrived. Now what?

I decide to drive around to scope out the island before choosing a hotel. I know from Pete Dye that Slater Babcock lives in a house on Admirals Lane and that his bar, the Drunken Dolphin, is on Duval Street.

I'll go to his house and bar as if on a surveillance stakeout. I've never met the young man, but I've seen digital photos of him and Hope together, taken by Hope's roommates: longish, sandy blond hair, regular features with a square jaw, blue eyes, a friendly smile, and the physique of an athlete. A handsome kid. Maybe he has a beard now, or long hair, like me. There is no chance that Slater would recognize me, even without my weathered, beachcomber look, which I've gotten to like; now, no one would mistake me for a corporate lawyer, a good thing. If Hope had shown him a family picture, he would never expect to see her father, not in Key West, not after all this time. If there were to be a confrontation with me, it would have happened long before now, Slater would likely assume.

First, Slater's house. I turn right off the causeway onto North Roosevelt Boulevard, pull into a gas station, and enter the address of Slater's house into the GPS. I'm directed by a woman's voice to take a left out of the gas station, proceed south along Roosevelt Boulevard, which becomes Truman Avenue after it crosses White Street, then right onto Whitehead Street, left onto Eaton Street, right onto Front Street— at this point I'm grateful that this GPS lady knows her way around town—and finally right onto Admirals Lane, a little semicircle near the northwestern end of the island.

I slow as I come to number 501, a single-story white cottage with a green tin roof and crushed shell driveway, and park across the street. The carport at Slater Babcock's house is empty; the green wooden hurricane shutters are propped open. What if I come back at three A.M. with a gas can and burn down the cottage, ideally with Slater Babcock in his bed? Would I be able to go back home, content that Hope had been avenged, even if Slater didn't know why he was dying? Would that end the matter?

Probably not. I would not have found out what happened to Hope. And I couldn't do something like that anyway, as Pete Dye has pointed out, and as Vernon Douglas certainly knows, too. No, whatever plan I can come up with, whatever revenge I may seek, needs to be something that does not make me no better than Slater Babcock. I sadly understand in that moment that solid-citizen Jack Tanner is sitting here in this rental car, still constrained by the rules of civilized society, and thus powerless to take any action that matters. But I'm here, so I need to find out what I can do, and what will happen as a result.

I check my notebook again for the address of the Drunken Dolphin, program it into the GPS, ease away from the curb and drive to Key West's main drag and prime tourist destination, with its restaurants, bars, shops, art galleries, souvenir stores, ice cream parlors, and hotels.

I follow the GPS lady's instructions and find Duval, then cruise slowly along the street, taking in the sights of this interesting little town (I guess I'm a tourist at heart). And then there's the Drunken Dolphin, a white one-story cinder-block structure with a flat roof. An adjoining lot has been converted into a beach volleyball court with a thatched tiki bar hut. I park the Taurus in a vacant space on the other side of the street, in front of the Almond Tree Inn, and watch customers enter and exit the bar for a while, then decide to go in for a drink and a look around: the showing-up-is-80-percent-of-life part of the game, with the remaining 20 percent a total crap shoot.

Inside, the Drunken Dolphin has an Old Key West motif: photos of Duval Street starting a century ago, judging by the horse carts, and then the automobiles, and look of the people. In some of the photographs, old-time fishing parties display their catches hanging on long stringers, and men wearing mustaches and straw boaters sit at a bar, not this one, and drink foamy draft beers, raising their mugs to the camera. Also on display are lobster pots, fishing nets with big cork floats, gaping shark jaws and more mounted game fish: big bulky tarpon, majestic sailfish and barracuda with mouthfuls of needle-sharp teeth.

The place is packed. "Margaritaville," the Jimmy Buffett anthem for the kick-back-in-the-tropics crowd, plays loudly on the sound system. I slide onto a barstool. After a moment, the bartender, a huge man with a ponytail and the dark skin of a native of some island somewhere, his arms covered with tattoos, comes over and asks, "What's your poison, sport?" He's wearing a red tank top and jeans.

I order a draft Red Stripe and scan the room. Tourist families—they don't look like natives of the Keys—sit at tables munching on platters of nachos and chicken wings and sipping drinks containing fruit and parasols. Lined up along the bar beside me are weathered men who could be fishing guides and tour-boat captains, and women who seem to be regulars, judging by their bantering with the bartender as they drink shots and beers, sans parasols.

All the usual suspects for a bar like this, but not the proprietor. I decide that I'll finish my beer and leave. I've come to the jackal's den and the jackal is not at home.

And then Slater Babcock pushes through the kitchen door and walks over to the end of the bar, not ten feet from where I'm sitting.

"Hey boss," the bartender calls out to him.

"Gimme a Bloody Mary," Slater says, nodding a hello to the customers he seems to know.

This is why I came, but still, I'm shocked, frozen in place, staring at him. He does have a beard now, and longer hair, a deep suntan, and a gold ring in his pierced left ear, but otherwise looks like the person in the photos. It's definitely him. He's wearing a black Bob Marley tee shirt, olive green cargo shorts, boat shoes with no socks, and a shark's tooth necklace: a frat boy on permanent spring break.

So here it is, the moment I've been anticipating all during this journey. For an entire year, really. I look at my heavy glass beer mug sitting in front of me on the bar. It could be a weapon. Or I could go out to the car and get Langdon's Derringer . . .

Slater walks over to the three girls standing at one end of the bar. As a responsible liquor license owner, he should check their IDs. None of them look to be of legal drinking age—or legal anything age. Instead, he begins chatting them up.

Girls like Hope.

I find myself standing next to him without knowing how I got there. One of the girls is laughing at something he said. Slater looks at me and smiles.

"Help you, sir?"

Yeah, he can help me. I'm shaking as I jam my finger into his chest.

"What did you do with my daughter?" I shout.

Slater takes a step backward and raises his hands.

"Hey, wait a minute, sir. Calm down . . ."

"Is there a problem, boss?" the big bartender asks Slater.

"Your daughter?" Slater says. "Who's that?"

The three girls have moved away from us.

"I'm Jack Tanner. Hope Tanner's father," I tell him.

Slater pauses, as if trying to remember who that is. And then: "Hope . . . Look, Mr. Tanner, I cared for Hope and, as I told the police, I have no idea what happened to her. I really don't."

I notice that the place is silent, everyone watching this drama play out.

"You're lying!" I shout and grab him by the shoulder. Then feel a big strong hand grab me by the bicep and pull me backward, away from Slater.

"It's okay, Mickey," Slater tells the bartender. "We're fine."

"We're *not* fine," I say.

"Look, Mr. Tanner, I'm very sorry for your loss," Slater says, "but I'll say again: I do not know what happened to Hope. And if you need anything else from me, you should contact my lawyer. But you should leave here now . . ."

I pause and Mickey grabs my arm again.

"Right now," he says. "Easy way or hard way."

I pause a moment longer, then turn and walk out of the bar, get into my car, and drive away, with no idea in the world where I'm going.

AFTER DRIVING around awhile, no destination in mind, wondering if I'm now done with Slater Babcock, and not knowing the answer, I check into the Casa Marina Resort on Reynolds Street, which looks like a nice place to stay.

The hotel, on the southern tip of the island, is a three-story yellow stucco building that looks like a grand old Spanish estate. In my room, which has an ocean view, I flop onto the bed, exhausted, and more pass out than fall asleep. I don't know how often I dream, because, if I do, I don't usually remember them. But later, I will remember this one.

A HURRICANE is battering Key West. Where the hell did that come from? There'd been no warning, at least none that I'd heard. Its name is Brenda. It's a level two, an intensity somewhere in that middle ground between ride it out, and mandatory evacuation.

The streets are deserted except for me as I make my way down Duval, soaked, storm-tossed, fighting the wind for forward motion. It's not clear why I haven't taken shelter.

A black-and-white Chevy Tahoe with Key West Police Department markings comes rolling slowly down Duval toward me. It pulls over to the curb with a short burst from its lights and siren. I look around: Who, me? There's no one else on the street.

The officer, who looks exactly like Vernon Douglas, powers down the window and says, "Hey Jack, what are you doing out in a storm like this? Hop in, I'll take you to a shelter."

I don't want to be taken to a shelter with other orphans of the storm. I know that I'm on a mission, even though it's not clear what the mission is. I make an effort to appear calm and reasonable, as calm and reasonable as a man can be who is out for a stroll in a level two hurricane. I walk over to the Tahoe, grabbing onto a parking meter with both hands for balance, and shout to be heard above the howling wind: "Hi Vernon. I'm on my way to a friend's house just around the corner."

Vernon looks at me, as if deciding whether to believe me or not, then replies, "Okay. Go directly there and stay inside."

"I will, thanks."

Thanks for not diverting me from my still-unknown mission.

Two more blocks down Duval, I reach a cinder block building with no sign announcing its name. This is my destination, I realize. The building is battened down with plywood nailed over the windows. The parking lot is deserted, except for six motorcycles blown over in a heap. No other signs of life.

I somehow know that there is a hurricane party inside. I push through the door to find that it's a bar packed with lively partygoers. A Jimmy Buffett song, "Surfing in a Hurricane," is playing on the sound system. Dripping water onto the floor, I scan the crowd.

Seated at a round table back near the kitchen entrance are the Devil's Disciples: Harold Whittaker, Alan Dupree, Miles Standish, Langdon Lamont, Victor Purcell, and the resurrected

Tom Jarvis. Harold notices me, and waves me over. In the world of dream logic, I'm not surprised to see them. Those were their motorcycles out in the parking lot.

Then I spot a young man standing at the far end of the bar with a group of three young women, one of whom looks like Hannah, laughing at whatever he's saying. The man has long, sandy blond hair, blue eyes, and a beard, and is wearing a Hawaiian shirt, jeans, and boat shoes. I don't know who this young man is, but I realize that he is evil and must be killed.

I approach him, grab his shoulder, and say, "Where is she?"

"What?" the man responds, turning to face me.

I shout, "Tell me what happened to my daughter!"

The man raises his hands, palms out, in a gesture of peace. "Hey, look buddy, if your daughter's here at the party, I'll be happy to . . ."

"You killed her!" I shout.

"Killed her? Now wait a minute, pal. Killed who?"

"My daughter!" I yell. "Hope Tanner!"

The man backs away from me and shrugs his shoulders as if he's never heard the name before. Enraged, I withdraw Langdon's Derringer from my pants pocket, which until then I didn't know I had, close the distance between us, press the barrel to the man's forehead, and say, "Admit it and I won't kill you."

"Hey, wait a minute . . ." he says, not moving.

I cock the little pistol.

"Wait . . . Wait . . . Okay, I did it. I killed her," he says, and starts to cry.

Through the din of the party I hear a familiar voice shout: "Jack! Hey Jack! Wait!"

Pete Dye is standing just inside the front door in a combat shooting stance, his pistol pointed toward the other end of the bar at the big bartender, who is leveling a shotgun at me.

Standoff.

I resolve it by pulling the Derringer's trigger. A metallic click. Not loaded! Then an orange-red flash from the shotgun barrel out ahead of the sound and Pete Dye firing too . . .

RIGHT AT that point a noise wakes me up. I look around, trying to get my bearings. The noise is a leaf blower outside the window. I stand up, move to the window, and watch the waves rolling up onto the beach. Desperate, hopeless, ashamed, I close my eyes, and for the first time in my life, utter the closest thing to a prayer I can manage:

Please. I want my family back.

18

I'll have lunch and then book a flight out of Miami and go home. Finally, I have the answer to what I'll do when I confront my daughter's killer: Nothing, nothing at all, except defeat him in my dreams. I don't know what will become of me when I get home, but there's no longer any reason to stay here. I am who I am.

I could get a sandwich at the hotel but instead, I'm not sure why, I drive back to Duval, park at a spot a good distance from the Drunken Dolphin, and notice a place called Crabby Dick's, with an outdoor patio. I get out of the car and go in, and ask the hostess for a table outside.

I'm looking over the menu as the waitress comes over to take my order. She's a pretty young girl wearing a skimpy white tee shirt with a Crabby Dick's parrot logo and tight white shorts.

The nameplate pinned on her tee shirt says Bonnie—but it's Hannah, the motorcycle thief.

Unfucking believable. Am I still dreaming?

She looks at me, and says, "Hey look, man, I'm sorry about what I did. Really sorry." She smiles. "But maybe I can make it up to you."

It *is* Hannah.

Now what should I do? These days, I never seem to know.

"Look, Jack, why don't we go to my apartment. It's nearby. I'll make you a sandwich, and we can talk."

"Where's my motorcycle?"

"Uh . . . I've got it. Come to my place and I'll give you the keys."

"Did you get it serviced?"

She looks confused, of course. Dumb question.

"Never mind. Okay, let's go."

Maybe I'm interested in hearing how a young girl went wrong. I couldn't save Hope, maybe I can somehow save Hannah, or whatever her name is. Or maybe I'm in such a bad state now that I'll do whatever anyone suggests.

HANNAH LIVES in a small, second-floor apartment above a tattoo parlor on Angela Street, around the corner and down two blocks from Crabby Dick's. When we're inside, she offers me a beer and then goes into the bedroom to change. I'm drinking it while looking out a window, which has a partial view of the water, when I hear her come out of the bedroom. I turn to find her smiling at me. She's nude.

So this is how she means to make it up to me. I know that many men, probably most men, would take her up on her offer, and call it even.

In fact, I'm taking a while telling her I'm not interested when she walks over, puts her arms around my neck and gives me an open-mouthed kiss on the lips. I'm speechless—not only because Hannah's tongue is in my mouth.

She ends the kiss and whispers into my ear. "Fuck me daddy . . . Fuck your little girl . . ."

Shocked, I push her away.

"*What* did you say?"

"Hey, take it easy. Older men always like that—the fuck-your-daughter thing. I could be your daughter's age, if you have one."

I grab her by the arm and shout, "Don't you say that to me!"

Still smiling, she says, "You like it rough, huh? Cuz we can do that . . ."

Right at that moment, the apartment door rattles open and a man enters. The man looks to be in his thirties, short and thin, with the small, dark eyes of a rat, and acne scars on his face. He's wearing a wife-beater tee shirt that reveals scrawny arms, dirty jeans, and cowboy boots. He holds a silver revolver in his right hand.

"Hey, dude," the man says, his grin revealing nicotine-stained teeth. "You tryin' to fuck my girl?"

"No, no," I tell him. "I was just . . ."

The man holds up his left hand, palm outward, to silence me.

"So you just came to deliver a pizza and found her buck naked like this?"

Hannah goes into the bedroom and closes the door as he says, "Whatever you're doin' here, dude, it's gonna cost you."

Hannah comes out of the bedroom, dressed in jeans and a halter top. "Hey, Jimmy, I kind of like this guy," she says. "Maybe we can work something out."

"What we're gonna work out, sweetie, is what we always work out," Jimmy answers. "We take cell phone photos of you two in bed together, you suckin' his cock, him fuckin' your ass, whatever works. Then, if he's been a good boy, he gets to leave, without his cash and credit cards."

Finally, I've had it. I will not allow this girl to scam me a second time.

"Not going to happen," I say, and walk out the door, without the keys to my Road King. Fortunately, Jimmy does not shoot me in the back.

IT REALLY is time to get the hell out of Key West before I kill someone, or someone kills me, or I go crazier than I apparently am. I gave it my best effort. Maybe that'll be enough to hang onto as I face the future. I'll get something to eat and then leave for home, even though I have no idea what I'll do when I get there, just as I had no idea what I'd do when I got to Key West. Wing it again, I suppose. As for Hannah, I wish her well, I really do. I think she must have had a rough childhood and is doing the best with what she has. If taking advantage of middle-aged guys like me is the only way for her to survive, then so be it.

I walk back over to Duval and notice a bar called Sloppy Joe's. No shortage of bars on this street. It's a two-story white stucco building with red brick pillars and the name of the establishment painted in big lettering on the top story, front and side. As good a place as any for lunch.

Inside, the flags of many countries hang from the ceiling. The place is crowded with people having a drink and lunch at the bar and at tables. The walls are covered with memorabilia from the bar's long history, most prominently a display of photos of the bar's most prominent former patron, Ernest Hemingway, whose presence looms large all over Key West. Hanging near the Hemingway gallery is a mounted blue marlin, similar to the one suspended from the hoist at the marina named for the majestic fish on Islamorada.

I locate a seat at the bar, scan a menu the bartender gives me, and order the two house specialties, a sloppy joe sandwich and, why not, a Papa Doble—"Papa's favorite!" the menu says, consisting of "Bacardí light rum, grapefruit juice, grenadine, splash of sweet & sour, club soda and fresh-squeezed lime, $6.75."

As I'm sipping my drink and waiting for my sandwich, a man seated at the bar beside me, and a woman next to him, finish their lunches and leave. When they do, a man takes the next stool over. He's wearing a tan, short-sleeved safari shirt and canvas shorts, with a length of rope for a belt, and white canvas deck shoes. Three long cigars are in one of his shirt pockets. He bears a striking resemblance to the photos of Ernest Hemingway on the walls.

"Like the Papa Doble?" the man asks, looking over at me.

THE BARTENDER, a portly man with red hair and beard, arrives to see if we need anything. I'm feeling relaxed and ask for another Papa Doble. My companion asks for another Daiquirí. As we sip our drinks, I introduce myself. The man, oddly, does not reciprocate, as if I'm supposed to know who he is.

19

His name is Edward Hollingsworth. We are aboard his boat, cruising the Gulf Stream off Key West at seven A.M. The boat is a white-hulled, twenty-eight-foot Hatteras named the *Pilar*. It is a lovely vessel, not at all like its namesake, Hemingway's thirty-eight-foot wooden cabin cruiser with a black hull, which sailed in these same waters in the 1930s when its owner was a Key West resident, Edward explained.

We've been hanging out together since we met at Sloppy Joe's. When I told Edward I was leaving on the day we met, he asked me to stay on in Key West a few more days. "Trust me, Jack, I think you'll find it interesting," he said. I told him I would, maybe because he seemed like an interesting person, maybe because I really had nothing to do back home. Maybe both.

That first night, we had dinner and lots of rum drinks at an oceanfront place Edward knows called Louie's Backyard. Midway through the meal, Edward said, "So, Jack, what brings you to Key West?"

"It's a very long story," I answered.

"Tell me anyway," he said. "I collect stories."

So I once again broke my vow of silence and told him the recent, sad history of the Tanner family.

We were seated outside on the patio, the wind off the Atlantic rustling the fronds on the palm trees, eating shrimp and grits Caribbean-style, which he recommended. He listened to me without saying anything until I finished, concluding the story with my confrontation with Slater Babcock at the Drunken Dolphin. Then he sat back in his chair, took a cigar and a lighter from his shirt pocket, and fired up the cigar, and slowly shook his head, a look of profound sadness in his eyes.

"I've known pain and loss, too, Jack," he said. "But that's no consolation. All you can do is keep breathing, and try to keep the black dog at bay."

I didn't know it then but later, via Google on a computer in the Casa Marina's business center, I learned that Hemingway called his depression "the black dog." He never overcame it. I don't know if I will or not.

Edward has been stingy with the details of his own life. He is a "retired businessman" who has lived all over the world; he enjoys hunting and fishing; he has had four wives and has three sons; he has a house in Idaho; he has been living aboard *Pilar* for the past few years, cruising "wherever my fancy and the Gulf Stream take me." Three cats live aboard *Pilar*, too; they are all named for French novelists—Zola, Rabelais, and Balzac—and came aboard of their own volition, one at a time, at various ports of call. I wonder if they have six toes, like Hemingway's cats did. I don't ask about this, but maybe will try to take a look sometime when I'm on the *Pilar*. Here, kitty, kitty . . .

I'm just familiar enough with Hemingway lore from reading a book about Key West before I began my trip to know that all of the details of Edward's life, as he has reported them, are similar—or identical—to those of the famous writer's. And, of course, he has made himself *look* like Hemingway. So Edward is either putting me on for some reason, putting everyone on, or he belongs at some place like The Sanctuary for treatment of his delusions.

No matter, I can use a friend, now that the Disciples are back home, someone with an upbeat personality and a certain *joie de vivre*, who can, at least for a little while, serve the same purpose as Jenna's medication does for her. And why hurry back to an empty house and no job?

This morning, it's blue water fishing, which I agreed to when Edward assured me that we'd follow a strict catch-and-release policy. That is, unless one of us hooked into "a real trophy." Then we'd have to talk, he said. I'm seated in *Pilar's* cockpit as Edward navigates out to a location where he believes that there just might be some tuna running.

An early fog has burned off; there is a light chop, not enough to make me seasick, which is a possibility if the wind picks up, causing *Pilar* to rock and bob more than it is right now. We have steaming mugs of good coffee Edward made in the galley. My mood has improved. I'm enjoying myself, out on the deep blue sea with an interesting companion, even if he is a total head case, and not simply a big-time Hemingway aficionado. Even if this is only palliative relief, I'm grateful for it. I wish Jenna were here too, for a dose of whatever it is I'm experiencing.

"I was thinking about inviting that kid, Slater Babcock, out for some fishing," Edward says above the wind and engine noise. "Who knows, he might hook into a big one that pulls him right in."

He's joking, of course. Isn't he? But maybe that's not a bad idea. Edward is maybe ten years older than me, but he is muscular, and a former amateur boxer, he said. More of the Hemingway résumé there; will he end up shooting himself with a shotgun to complete the act? If so, I hope I'm not around. With Edward as my wingman, maybe I'll be able to confront Slater in a more meaningful way than I did at the Drunken Dolphin. I certainly couldn't do any worse.

"Look," Edward exclaims, pointing to the front of the boat, where two dolphins are riding the bow waves. "That's good luck, you know."

I hear a whirring noise behind me. Edward swivels his chair to look and calls out, "Fish on! Fish on!" One of the four fishing rods, mounted on the stern in chrome sleeves and rigged for trolling, is bent under the weight of something big, and line is running out fast. Edward powers down the twin engines and yells, "Go for it, Jack! Grab that rod! You're in for a fight, that's for sure!"

When the big fish makes a leap, I see it's a blue marlin. It does not want to be caught; he tests my resolve and my arms and shoulders for more than an hour as he dives deep, then breaks the surface to dance on his tail, as Edward expertly maneuvers the boat and keeps shouting, "Tip up! Keep the goddamned tip up or you'll lose him!"

It feels like I've hooked Moby Dick. Edward repeatedly asks me if I want him to take over the rod, just long enough to give me a rest, but I always decline, feeling that somehow fighting this fish is the most important thing I've ever done. Finally, just as my arms feel like they are being pulled out of my shoulder sockets, the fish begins to tire, and remains on the surface for a longer time, not diving so deep.

"You've got 'im!" Edward calls out, backing the boat slowly toward the fish. "Tip up and reel in that big boy. Steady now, Jack, he's yours to lose!"

When the marlin is alongside, Edward puts the engines in neutral, comes down to the deck, pulls on leather work gloves, grabs the steel leader on the line, and lifts the head of the fish up, gently, being careful of the long, sharp sword, as if he is going to kiss it.

"A beauty," he says, as he holds the leader with one hand and takes a pair of pliers out of the back pocket of his shorts. "Maybe six hundred pounds. Not trophy size, that's over a thousand, and I have caught some that size and more, so no problem here, we'll put him back and let him grow some more."

He looks directly into one of the marlin's big round blue eyes and says, "I'll be baa-aack! Ha!" Then he uses the pliers to remove the barbless hook from the fish's mouth, leans over the transom and massages the fish's belly. After a while, he puts his hands on the marlin's back and pushes him slowly away from the boat. I watch as the fish floats motionless for several minutes, wondering if he's dying. Then he shakes himself and, with a whip of his tail, is gone beneath the shimmering surface of the Gulf Stream. I hope the fish will be smarter or luckier or still too small for trophy size the next time he comes across a hook in the water.

"That was a very good catch," Edward says, smiling. "You know the quote, 'Anyone can be a fisherman in May'? That's from *The Old Man and the Sea*. The book was written in Cuba. You should read it if you're going to do more of this blue water stuff. Hemingway could have been referring to this month, too. But in July, when the big ones run deep, anyone *cannot* be a fisherman. More than anything, including luck, it takes persistence, and most people don't have it. It's very similar to finishing a novel, which is a distance run and not a sprint and why so many people who start one never make it to the end."

He takes two cans of Foster's Lager from an ice chest under one of the bench seats, pops the tops, and hands one to me.

"You know what the Old Man, whose name was Santiago, says as he's fighting his marlin? 'Fish, I love you and respect you very much. But I will kill you dead before this day ends.' Now that's some damn fine writing, don't you think? You get that by starting with one true sentence, and then you write another, and another, and finally you have a book of fiction that's truer than real life. That's the secret to telling a good story, Jack!"

I nod as if I know what Edward is talking about and drink down half the can of Foster's in one swallow, foam bubbling down my chin. I wipe off the foam with the back of my hand and say, "It *was* a nice fish, wasn't it?"

Edward unrigs the four rods, lays them on the deck, goes below, and comes back with two long cigars. He gives me one of them and says, "Arturo Fuentes. Let's have a victory smoke, just like good old Red Auerbach." Red, I know, was the legendary coach of the Boston Celtics, and he always lit up a cigar after a victory.

Then Edward climbs up into the captain's chair, lights his cigar with a Zippo from his pocket, and offers me the flame, which I accept. The tips of the cigars already are snipped off. He savors a long puff and says, "Let's head back to the barn, counselor. That's quite enough fun for one morning, I'd say."

Iт's noon. *Pilar* is moored at a dock at the Key West Bight Marina. Bone weary after my marlin encounter, I'm below deck taking a nap on the stateroom bunk when I'm awakened by the clanging of the ship's bell and the captain's voice calling out, "Lunch!" Clang-clang-clang! "Lunch is served!"

I see that all three cats have been napping with me on the bunk. I scratch one, a calico, behind its ears, then hold up its paw: six toes. Also awakened by the bell, the cats stretch, hop off the bunk, and walk up the stairway; apparently it's their lunchtime, too. I follow them.

Edward is cooking two grouper fillets on a small gas grill. "Just bought these off a commercial fishing boat right here at the marina," he tells me. "They were swimming just a few hours ago. Can't get any fresher. Do you know that all the supposedly fresh fish you get inland were in fact frozen?" I didn't.

To accompany the grouper, there is a mango and avocado salad with lemon vinaigrette dressing, a loaf of crusty French bread, and more Red Stripe from the ice chest. Among his other talents, Edward is a gourmet cook. He said he came to appreciate good food while living in Paris as a young man; years later, when he could afford it, he went back to study at Le Cordon Bleu culinary school. I wish I could introduce him to Marissa Kirkland, then eat a meal they jointly prepared. He still has not been specific about what business or businesses he's undertaken, saying only, "Oh, this and that over the years, some of which still generate royalties."

He's been interested in every small detail of Hope's disappearance and the ensuing events, with a particular interest in why I believe that Slater Babcock is responsible. When I asked him, as I did Vernon Douglas, what he would do in a similar circumstance, Edward thought about it for a while, and replied, enigmatically, "Oh, I never know the ending of a story until I get there and see what the characters themselves want to do. We're not there yet with your story, Jack. But trust me, we're getting close."

20

Edward and I hang out together for the next several days. This time spent with the man who thinks he's a deceased writer is like attending an Outward Bound school. There is more fishing, this time a full day of fly casting for bonefish from a flat-bottomed skiff which Edward poles around the backwaters while standing on a raised seat in the rear of the boat. Edward rented the skiff at a marina where he bought live shrimp for bait; the fly rods and tackle came off *Pilar*. There is skeet shooting at a gun range on Big Coppitt Key. Edward, I'm not surprised, is an expert with a shotgun; the two shotguns and shells also came off his boat. I manage to hit only two of the clays, which draws high praise from my companion. There is snorkeling on the reefs off Key West, which are teeming with sea life, including several sharks that glide—too close for comfort—below us. There is a sightseeing cruise aboard *Pilar* to the Dry Tortugas, a group of islands seventy miles west of Key West, where we see all kinds of birds.

"The Dry Tortugas National Park is home to two hundred twenty-nine species," Edward informs me. "It's my goal to see 'em all. So far, I've identified less than a third of that number."

He wishes he could take me wild boar hunting at a hunting preserve he knows up near Lake Okeechobee, he says, but there isn't time. I don't know why there isn't time, but I don't want to either kill or be killed by a wild boar, so no problem with that.

And if there were more time, Edward says—making me wonder again what sort of deadline Edward has—he'd take me on a cruise to Cuba. He knows a number of clandestine spots where we could drop *Pilar*'s anchor, swim ashore, and "pick up some Cohibas, Havana Club rum, and mami chulas," the latter of which, I assume, has something to do with female companionship. And there is more drinking, fine dining, and cigar smoking, with me sometimes sleeping in my room at the Casa Marina Resort, sometimes in a bunk aboard *Pilar*, and sometimes not at all.

Two nights ago, Edward surprised me by getting very drunk in a bar called The Golden Parrot. He always had more than a few drinks, but this night he seemed to be in a dark mood, and downed more than usual, not Daiquirís, but straight gin. He seemed to not know me, and began talking to himself, mostly unintelligibly. When the bartender refused to serve him any more drinks, Edward yelled something at him in what I think was Spanish, and tried to take a swing at him, across the bar. He missed and fell off his stool onto the floor, passed out.

"I'll take him home," I told the bartender, who just shrugged. I paid for our drinks and left a big tip. Being a bartender at The Golden Parrot on the Key West waterfront is quite a bit different from being the bartender at the Edina Country Club, whose name is Charlie, and who would have called the police.

I took Edward to his boat in a taxi. He staggered down the dock, my arm around his shoulders, and nearly fell onto the *Pilar*'s deck, catching himself on a railing. I tucked him into his bunk and left as he was already snoring.

The next morning, over café con leche and chicken and mushroom empanadas at the Cuban Coffee Queen on Margaret Street, Edward was in great spirits. He talked about hunting bighorn sheep in Idaho and where to get the best abalone "on the planet" (Sam's Grill in San Francisco). He did not mention what happened at The Golden Parrot the previous night. I'd been wondering if Edward had a dark side, and now I knew that he did.

From time to time, we spot Slater Babcock around town. "Hhmm," Edward says on the first sighting, when Slater is playing in a beach volleyball game. "Too bad you can't see inside a man, to see what stuff he's made of. Can't tell that until you test him under pressure and see how he behaves."

True enough. I've been tested under pressure and do not like the way I've behaved.

The following morning, I awaken in my hotel room, feeling like you are supposed to feel after a Conch Republic bacchanal. I shower, have orange juice and coffee in the hotel coffee shop, and decide to walk the three miles to the marina where *Pilar* is moored. The walk will help clear my head. I plan to tell Edward that I've decided to go to Slater Babcock's house this morning and, finally, to make him tell me about Hope. Apparently, Edward's subtle attempts to teach me what it means to be a real man have worked.

If Slater isn't there, I'll find him. I'll have Langdon's Derringer in my pocket. I'll do whatever is necessary to get to the truth. Edward will want to accompany me, but I'll decline, saying this is something I must do on my own. Surely, Edward will understand that. I could go right from the hotel to Slater's house. But I want to see Edward first, just in case something happens and I'm unable to see my new friend and mentor one last time.

I FIND Edward standing on the dock beside *Pilar,* spraying the hull with a hose attached to a faucet.

"I want to talk to you about something," I tell him.

"Sure, let's go aboard and chat over coffee," he says, and steps down onto the deck. I begin to follow him down the stairs leading to the galley when he says, "Wait here, I'll be back in a sec."

"It's a perfect morning," he says when he reappears with two mugs. "Let's take a little cruise and you can tell me what's on your mind."

"I don't have time for that," I tell him. "I've decided to talk to Slater Babcock about Hope."

"He's not at his house, or at the bar," Edward says.

I'm confused. "How do you know that?" I ask.

"Trust me, Jack. I know. Let's put out into the straits and I'll tell you all about it."

As always, Edward is a riddle, wrapped in a mystery, inside an enigma, to quote Winston Churchill speaking about the Soviet Union's national interest. But no sense in chasing after Slater if he's not around. I help cast off the lines and follow Edward up to the bridge. He starts the engines and eases away from the dock.

When we've been cruising for about twenty minutes, Edward checks the depth finder, cuts the engines and pushes a button that lowers the bow anchors.

"Forty feet under the hull here," he says. "A perfect spot."

I follow him down from the bridge.

"Wait here," he says, and goes into the main cabin. I hear a commotion, and then am shocked to see Slater Babcock come up the ladder from the galley, followed by Edward, who is holding a shotgun, the same one he used for skeet shooting. Slater's hands are tied behind his back with nylon rope, and there is a strip of duct tape across his mouth. He is wearing a Ramones tee shirt, khaki shorts, and boat shoes, and he is clearly terrified.

Edward pushes Slater into one of the fighting chairs on the stern.

"All right, Jack," he says. "You want to talk to Slater Babcock. He's ready to listen. I woke him from a sound sleep at six A.M."

He rips the duct tape off of Slater's mouth, causing him to wince.

"Are you fucking crazy?" Slater shouts. "Who the hell *are* you people? You kidnapped me! You're in a lot of trouble!"

"It appears to me that you are the one in trouble, Mr. Babcock," Edward says.

"What did you do to her?" I ask him again, this time with considerably more leverage to force an answer I'll accept. "You killed her, didn't you, you slimy little son of a bitch!"

I'm trembling, light-headed, breathing rapidly. Maybe I'm having a heart attack.

Slater begins to stand but Edward pushes him back with the barrel of the shotgun. "Easy now," Edward says. "Just sit there for a while, boy, and we'll see where we go from here."

"Look, Mr. Tanner, like I said, I really don't know, I swear," Slater says. "I liked her . . ."

"You're lying!" I shout, all the months of anger and frustration coming out. "You worthless little fuck!"

I move toward him with clenched fists, but Edward steps in front of me.

"You know," Edward says, "I don't think that the kid is ready yet for an honest exchange of information."

He points over the starboard bow.

"Cuba is twenty miles that way. The Guantanamo Bay Naval Base is at the southeastern end of the island. If we were having this conversation there, we might employ what our government calls enhanced interrogation techniques. But we are not there, so we'll have to improvise."

He levels the shotgun at Slater.

"Stand up."

Slater doesn't move. Edward jacks a shell into the shotgun's breech.

"Wait!" Slater shouts, and stands. "I didn't do anything to her. I told the police everything I know. I'm not lying."

He looks at me. "Please, Mr. Tanner, you gotta believe me . . ."

"Untie his hands," Edward tells me.

I step over to Slater, who turns around. I untie the rope and step back as Slater rubs his wrists.

"Good," Edward says. "Now take off your tee shirt."

"What?"

"The tee shirt. Take it off. I like the Ramones. Be a shame to ruin that shirt."

Slater takes it off and drops it on the deck. I see that he's wearing the shark's tooth necklace he had on when I met him in his bar.

"Look at that," Edward says. "Bad timing, you wearing that necklace."

"Huh?" Slater says.

"Never mind. Open the top of that seat behind you," he says to Slater. "It's an ice chest."

Slater does.

"Now reach in, take out some pieces of the meat and throw them overboard."

Again, Slater does as he's told, tossing bloody hunks of raw meat into the water.

"You know, Jack, I've caught some sharks on this spot," Edward says. "Hammerheads, black tip reef sharks, tigers . . . Other than great whites, tigers are the most dangerous. Seem to have a real taste for human flesh."

As the hunks of meat float on the surface, I watch for fins to appear. Slater watches, too.

"Look over there," Edward says, pointing toward the bow. Two fins are cutting the water's surface. "Just dolphins, having a romp. They're not man-eaters."

I look at Edward.

"What exactly are we doing here?" I ask him. "I mean, where's this going, Edward?"

"We're writing an end to your story, Jack," he tells me with a smile. "In fact, that's what we've been doing ever since we met at Sloppy Joe's."

He looks at Slater, who has finished his chumming and is standing there with bloody hands, looking distraught, as if he's just dug his own grave. Maybe he has.

"Okay, Mr. Babcock, now jump overboard," Edward says to him. "But I'll take that shark's tooth necklace before you do. It's a nice one." He laughs. "Plenty more where that came from, as you're about to find out."

"What?" Slater exclaims. "You're crazy! I'm not . . ."

Before he can finish, Edward fires a shell into the air above Slater's head, causing us both to jump.

"I mean it, young man. I want you in the water while we continue our conversation."

"No, I can't," Slater says, starting to cry. "I'm afraid . . . You're making a big mistake . . ."

Edward points the shotgun directly at Slater's chest, jacks in another shell, and says, "You're going in the water, alive or dead. All the same to me."

Slater is shaking and whimpering. I notice a wet stain spreading on the front of his khaki shorts. He's urinated on himself. He falls to his knees, head down, as if waiting for execution by beheading.

Edward takes a step toward him and says, "Dead then."

Slater looks at him, his face drained of color, terrified, eyes wide, as if he's looking at a ghost.

Hemingway's ghost.

"No, please . . ." he moans.

Edward's finger moves onto the trigger . . .

"Wait!" I tell him. "I don't want this." I pause, and realize I'm crying too. "Hope wouldn't want this . . ."

Edward lowers the shotgun and smiles.

"Okay, Jack, your call. Thing is, with enhanced interrogation techniques, the subjects either tell you the truth to get you to stop, or they lie and tell you what you want to hear to get you to stop. It takes a trained interrogator like they have at Gitmo over there to tell the difference. And even they aren't sure a good deal of the time. I think our friend here would confess to anything just to stay in the boat, wouldn't you, Mr. Babcock?"

Slater looks at us, apparently trying to decide what is the right answer.

"Yes," he finally says, looking as if he's about to faint. Then to me: "But I didn't hurt Hope. I'd never do anything like that."

"Let's head for the barn," Edward says. "Slater, go below and clean yourself up. Stay there until we reach port. Take a nice hot shower, and pour yourself a drink. You can borrow a pair of my shorts if you like, in the dresser in the stateroom. They'll be too big, but at least they're dry."

As Edward operates the electric hoist to raise the anchor, some of the chunks of meat floating on the surface of the water begin to disappear as fish begin to take them. I notice fins circling the area, and I don't think they're dolphins.

On the way in, I sit silently in the chair on the bridge. Edward, at the helm, is smoking a cigar. When we reach the Key West channel markers, he says, "That's what revenge looks like, Jack. I've had some experience with it. It can be pretty ugly, and usually, it's unsatisfying. Contrary to what you might think, it doesn't make you feel any better. If you're a good man, it can add to your pain. I frankly don't recommend it."

Two dolphins are riding our bow waves.

"Look," Edward says, pointing at them. "That's good luck."

He takes a long puff on the cigar and says, "If you told me this morning you were going home without trying to see Slater again, I wouldn't have brought him up on deck. No telling exactly how that was going to go, so best to avoid the situation if possible."

"Would you have actually fed him to the sharks?"

"That was entirely up to you, Jack. In all my stories, I always let the characters dictate what happens. Quite often, they surprise me by what they do."

"So I'm just a character in one of your stories?"

"Not just *a* character. In this story, you are the *main* character. And I'll say that you have exhibited considerable grace under pressure, which is one of the measures of a man."

"If Slater confessed, he just would've denied everything later," I say. "You were pointing a shotgun at him . . ."

Edward reaches into the pocket of his canvas shorts and comes out with a micro tape recorder.

"I would have had it all on here. Sure, he could have claimed he confessed under duress, but it would've been fun to see him stand trial."

"What happens now?" I ask as Edward slows to no-wake speed in the Key West harbor channel.

"Well, guilty or not, Slater Babcock goes on being Slater Babcock, you go home, do what you can to put your life back together, and I move on to the next port of call. It's time."

"But Slater will report us to the police."

"I've thought about that," Edward says, turning out of the channel toward the marina. "The thing is, I happen to know that his bartender is dealing drugs from right there in the Drunken Dolphin. Before I send Slater on his way, I'll suggest that he forgets about this cruise, and I'll forget that I know about the oxycodone you can get at his place without a prescription, as well as the coke and dexies and bennies, and the Rohypnol. Ever heard of that one? They call it the date rape drug. My info is that our Mr. Babcock regularly has his bartender slip it into the drinks of young girls, some of them underage. I think he'll develop a case of amnesia about the events of this fine morning." He looks over at me. "You should, too."

"How do you know all that?" I ask.

Edward smiles.

"Oh, I've spent a lot of time in Key West. People tell me things, just like you did. As I said, I'm a good listener."

21

The next morning, I'm in my room at the Casa Marina, just out of the shower, ready to drive back to Miami, when there's a knock on the door. I open it and am surprised to see Pete Dye.

"Hi Jack," he says. "Mind if I come in?" I have no idea how Pete found me and I don't ask him about this, because it's what he does.

FIVE HOURS later, Delta flight 2522 lifts off the runway at Miami International, bound for Minneapolis-Saint Paul International. I'm in seat 3A and Pete Dye is in 3C, no one between us.

Pete brought the stunning news that Hope's killer is buried in a cemetery on the grounds of the South Dakota State Penitentiary in Sioux Falls.

The day before his scheduled execution by lethal injection, Lyle Cutler, a fifty-five-year-old former guidance counselor at Central High School in Rapid City, told his minister that he'd accepted Jesus as his Savior and confessed to the murder of Annie Knox, a seventeen-year-old Central High student, for which he'd been convicted. He also admitted that he'd murdered four other girls over the past twelve years, including Hope Tanner. He said he wanted to tell the warden the same thing "so he won't feel badly about giving me the needle, because I deserve to die for what I've done."

Right about that. I wouldn't feel badly about giving him the needle. He is truly a devil, and all that can be done about such genetic mutants is to catch and cage or kill them.

After an audience with the warden, Cutler, with his lawyer present, told representatives from the governor's attorney general's offices that he frequently visited admissions offices at Midwestern colleges and universities as part of his duties as a guidance counselor. He'd been doing this for twenty-two years. He said that, beginning eight years earlier, a voice in his head sometimes told him to randomly choose and murder girls "as a lesson to all schoolgirls to obey their parents, do their homework and not act like sluts or they'll end up like the dead girls."

It was later discovered that he'd been treated for schizophrenia most of his adult life, but he had not disclosed this to his employer. He'd never been married. He had a brother and two sisters but, when notified by the warden of his impending execution, they said that they did not wish to attend or to claim their brother's body.

After Cutler confessed to the murders, Pete told me, the governor stayed his execution until he was able to lead police to the places he'd buried his victims other than Annie Knox, whose body had been found in a drainage ditch in a farm field outside Rapid City by a farmer training his dog to hunt.

Hope, who Cutler identified as "that Madison college girl," was buried in a proverbial shallow grave under a live oak tree in a stand of woods about ten miles north of the campus. Cutler said that he was just driving around the campus neighborhood after having dinner following a visit to the university when he saw a pretty girl walking alone. On an impulse, he asked her if she wanted a ride. She didn't, so he grabbed her.

Shuffling along in handcuffs and ankle shackles, he led a team of FBI agents and Wisconsin State Patrol officers to the site. Vernon Douglas was there, too. When Hope's body was found, it was transported to the Dane County Medical Examiner's Office and identified by dental records on file with the police department. Hope had a wisdom tooth extracted by a Madison dentist, who forwarded a copy of her record to the police after he learned about her disappearance. Vernon Douglas added the record to Hope's file.

When I didn't answer Vernon's calls to my house or cell phone, and did not return voicemail messages, and Douglas could not otherwise locate me, having learned from my law firm that I was no longer employed there, he called Pete Dye, whom he'd gotten to know during the investigation.

When Pete told me that Cutler had confessed to Hope's murder, I asked for the details.

"I'll tell you if you insist," Pete responded, "but please don't."

Pete is a good man, so I didn't. He later provided one final report to me about Slater Babcock. He sold his bar and left Key West for parts unknown. I do regret what he's been through, being a suspect in a murder case, and then that boat ride with Edward and me. I thought about calling him to apologize, but I delayed that call until Pete reported that he was gone.

Because of all the news coverage, Slater must know about Lyle Cutler, and Hope, and the other girls. Maybe he left because he was bored with Key West. But I wouldn't blame him if he wanted to make certain that Edward Hollingsworth could never find him again, even though it's been proven that he's an innocent man—or at least innocent of the murder of my daughter. Maybe, wherever he is, he dreams about swimming with sharks.

22

At eight o'clock on a chilly April Saturday morning, under a cloudless sky, I'm sitting on a patio chair in the backyard of our Edina house, wearing one of my lawyer uniforms: a navy blue pinstriped suit, white shirt, red tie, and black tasseled loafers. Birds are chirping their morning songs. Water droplets on the lawn glisten in the sunshine.

Jenna comes out of the house, looking great in a black silk suit, white blouse, black heels, and a pearl necklace and earrings. She is carrying two steaming mugs of coffee. She hands one to me and sits in the other chair.

"We'll get through today," she says.

"Okay."

"Really, we will, Jack."

"I know . . ."

And, at that moment, with Jenna beside me, I do know that we will.

THREE DAYS after arriving home, I went to The Sanctuary and told Jenna about Hope. I'd spoken by phone to her doctor first, and he told me that, in his opinion, Jenna could handle the news, and was ready to go home, as long as she made an appointment with a psychiatrist in Minneapolis he recommended, and continued her course of medication, modified as appropriate over time. All that was necessary was for Jenna to decide she was ready to leave The Sanctuary, he said.

We sat on a wooden bench beside a large pond as I told her what had happened to our daughter. We hugged, and cried together. Then Jenna told me a story.

A couple weeks before my visit, she was sitting on this same wooden bench when she was startled by a voice behind her: "Hi, Jenna, mind if I join you?"

She turned to see another patient, Gerald Manville, standing there. He was wearing pajamas and a robe, with bare feet, and was unshaven. She'd never seen him like that before; he had always been well-dressed and clean-shaven.

"Please do, Gerald," she replied. "This is such a peaceful spot."

Gerald was a man about her age, Jenna told me, who was a professor of art history at Dartmouth, and a painter. I noticed that Jenna spoke of him in the past tense. She didn't know why he was at The Sanctuary. Patients never talked to one another about their particular maladies. It was considered to be too sensitive a subject, and, she said, impolite.

She didn't know if he was married, or if he was straight or gay; she felt she might be stereotyping him because he is, or was, an artist. He was tall, and thin as a fence post, with an angular, off-kilter face that suggested a Picasso painting. He was intelligent and charming.

Once, he invited her to his room to see his paintings. She reflexively said a polite no, not knowing if it was art or sex he had in mind, and he never asked again, so she didn't know how good a painter he was, or if the résumé he'd recounted to her was real. Maybe he was a housepainter. Didn't matter, she liked him.

Gerald took a dinner roll out of the pocket of his robe and began tossing crumbs toward a squirrel that was sitting on its haunches, watching them.

"So, Jenna," he said, "another day in the cuckoo's nest."

Then he tossed the rest of the roll to the squirrel, stood up, sighed, and walked into the lake.

"By the time I was able to alert the staff, it was too late," Jenna told me. "Back in my room, I looked into the bathroom mirror, and said, 'I am *not* like that. I will *not* be like that.'"

And at that moment, Jenna said as we sat by the pond, she knew she could go home soon. She was thinking about just showing up to surprise me when I called to say I was coming for her.

"You know, I've been thinking about Edward Hollingsworth," Jenna says as we sit together on our patio. I told her all about Edward on the flight home from The Sanctuary, and, during our first days at home, about everything else that happened in Key West, and during my trip down there.

"Maybe he was Hemingway's ghost," she says as we sit in the backyard with our coffee. "Or maybe a guardian angel sent to help you, taking that particular human shape because it was Key West."

"I like to think that he was one of those, and not just some delusional Looney Tunes," I say. "He helped me more than I can say."

"Do you remember that old song we liked?" Jenna says. "About how Oz never gave anything to the Tin Man he didn't already have?" She squeezes my hand. "That guy didn't teach you anything about being a man you didn't already know. I wonder where he is now."

I look up at the window of Hope's room, as if expecting to see my daughter's smiling face through the glass.

"Before Pete Dye and I drove to Miami, I stopped at the marina to say good-bye. His boat was gone. The dock master said he paid his bill that morning and left. He told me Edward shows up every year or so, stays awhile, then just disappears. He gave me a note from him, handwritten on stationery from the Hotel Ambos Mundos in Havana. It said that if I ever wanted to get in touch with him, just put a note in a bottle and drop it into any body of water that flows to the sea, and he'll get it."

"I love that," Jenna says. "And I believe it."

Three deer, a doe and two spotted fawns, wander into our yard and pause.

"Look at that," Jenna says. "A family."

So DID I accomplish anything by riding from Edina to Key West on a motorcycle? More accurately, on two motorcycles and in a rental car? I've concluded that, even though fate had already dictated the result of my hunt for my daughter's killer, I'm glad I did make the trip because I learned some valuable things I didn't know, after fifty-two years on the planet:

When overcome by self-doubt, and feeling lost, it's important that you do *something*, even if you discover later that it wasn't exactly the right thing.

Motorcycles are fun, but there is a trade-off between the exhilaration of the ride, and the possibility that you could, at any moment, be killed or injured. So the best way to enjoy it is to achieve a state of denial.

Never be tempted to own a bed-and-breakfast, unless you're married to a woman like Marissa Kirkland—and, even then, don't.

Student life at the University of Wisconsin, as at all schools, renews itself each fall with a new crop of students; past tragedies do not live on in the collective consciousness. True about life in general.

Do not pick up hitchhikers, especially pretty young girls.

Not all motorcycle gangs are what they appear.

Savannah is a lovely city, worth another visit, if only for the food at Mama Sally's.

Daytona Beach during Bike Week is not worth another visit.

They mean it when they say that the professional drivers section in a truck-stop restaurant is for professional drivers only.

On the road, you can encounter random acts of kindness, as well as sudden violence, same as off the road.

The bad part about being fired from Hartfield, Miller, Simon & Swensen is not my former partners' lack of appreciation for all the hours of my life I gave to the firm. It is that I took those hours from my family.

People mainly do not change, only their circumstances do.

Travel for purposes of self-renewal should be fully deductible.

You can forget, for varying intervals of time, about most any problem you might have. But when your child dies, you never forget that, even for a moment.

And sometimes, to get home, you have to ride away from home.

THE SERVICE for Hope is at First Lutheran Church in Edina, the Reverend Lars Johansen presiding. Jenna and I attended Sunday services at First Lutheran just often enough to maintain our status as "social Lutherans," meaning that we came on Advent Sunday, Christmas Eve, Easter, and one other Sunday every month or so.

I've always considered church membership analogous to belonging to the right clubs in terms of business networking. But now I understand that, for many people, being part of a congregation comforts them and helps them get through hard times.

In attendance today are friends and family, many of whom have come from out of town, as well as Pete Dye, Vernon Douglas, all of my former law partners who were available, whom I welcome warmly and with gratitude, and, representing the Boston chapter of the Devil's Disciples, Harold Whittaker and Langdon Lamont. The other remaining Disciples had commitments they couldn't break, but sent their condolences, and generous donations to a charity we had named in lieu of flowers, a scholarship fund at the University of Wisconsin endowed in our daughter's name. Hank and Lauren Whitby are among the contingent of friends—Hank, the neighbor whose manly approach to life I've always admired. As I greeted him and thanked him for coming, he gave me a very firm handshake and said, "You're a good man, Jack. I greatly admire how you handled all this." That was nice. It was as if he were pinning a medal on my chest.

Hope is here at the church, too, resting in a cherry wood casket set upon a rolling metal bier in front of the altar. The casket is closed of course, our poor sweet baby, her lovely face never to be looked upon again in this world. Sunlight streaming through a stained glass window illuminates a display of photographs of Hope showing her growing from infancy until she is nineteen years old, forever.

Jenna and I do get through it: Reverend Johansen's remarks about our family, the soaring choir music, words of remembrance from me, loving comments from Jenna, tearful readings of scriptures by Hope's friends.

On the way here, Jenna mentioned that maybe we'd like to start attending church regularly. I said yes, I think that would be nice. After all, I didn't say, my prayer back in Key West has been answered. The Tanner family is back together again.

At Crystal Lake Cemetery, Hope Tanner is interred in a grave located between two others; I've just purchased all three. An old live oak tree stands nearby. I wonder if a squirrel family lives in the tree. It should be raining, I think. I want lightning, rain, and thunder. A raging of the heavens. The day is too nice for this.

The graveside service is unspeakably hard, as it must be when, in a fracturing of nature's plan, parents lay a child to rest. I realize, sitting with Jenna in the front row of folding chairs, that this place, and not Key West, is the true end of my journey.

I won't say any more about it than that. If you haven't been through such a horrible thing, I wouldn't want you to suffer vicariously. If, God forbid, you have, I wouldn't want you to relive it.

When the service is finished, and all we mourners are walking toward our cars, on the way to our house for food and drink, I'm surprised to find that there is enough left of me to survive.

Just enough. I'm running on fumes.

Jenna seems to be holding up pretty well through all of this, though I don't for the life of me know how. I've heard religious people say that God never gives you more suffering than you can bear. Jenna and I are going to find out if that's true.

23

A perfect August morning in Edina. A moving van is pulling away from our Maitland Avenue house, with all our possessions, the accumulation of a family's lifetime, so far, packed inside, as Jenna and I watch from the front porch, holding hands.

I've gotten a job on the faculty of the University of Michigan Law School, my alma mater, to teach a course in tax law. The dean's office had sent e-mails about the position to all graduates practicing tax law in the private and public sectors. I was one of thirty applicants, but the only one to have been editor of the law review. Aided by a strong recommendation from the managing partner at Hartfield, Miller, and perhaps, I suspect, also by knowledge about my family's history, I was hired.

At Jenna's suggestion, I am keeping my hair longer than usual, but shorter than it was when I got home from Key West, and have kept the beard, now neatly trimmed. She said I look "more professorial" that way.

Jenna has been doing well. We do not have "closure." I can't even comprehend what that word might mean to us. Jenna's doctor in Minneapolis has recommended a colleague in Ann Arbor. A blessed if fragile optimism has returned to our lives, optimism that Jenna and I can find peace, and even a growing measure of contentment, as we soldier on through the coming years.

Maybe that's all anyone can hope for. Maybe that's enough.

It's hard for Jenna and me to leave the home where we raised Hope, and have had so many good times, and treasured memories, but my unemployment and Jenna's hospital bills have put a serious strain upon our finances, and it will be good to get a paycheck again. I'd always thought about someday leaving the daily grind of corporate law practice to teach, so I'm excited to begin my new job; academia will be my refuge.

We've promised friends and neighbors we will return to visit. We told that to Hope, too, at the cemetery, early this morning. And someday, we told our daughter, we will come back to stay with her, forever.

Of course, Hope will always be with us, wherever we are. When I got the law school job, Jenna and I flew to Detroit and drove a rental car, another Ford Taurus, to Ann Arbor. After three days of looking at houses with a real estate agent, a pleasant woman in her fifties named Harriett, we found a smaller version of our Edina house on a quiet street within walking distance of the law school.

We knew before we went inside that it was the one for us. It is a three-bedroom, four-bath, white colonial, twenty years newer than our Edina house, with "great curb appeal and a highly desirable location for resale," Harriett had said. It was owned by a university history professor and his wife; he got a job as department chair at the University of Pennsylvania. Open floor plan; remodeled kitchen with granite countertops and center island, and gas appliances; finished basement; attached two-and-a-half-car garage (room for a motorcycle, Jenna noted); a big backyard with mature trees, flower beds, and a white wooden arbor with flowering vines; walls of bookcases; and a U of M "Go Blue!" toilet seat in the first-floor powder room. All the right stuff for our new life.

During our first tour of the house, we were up on the second floor, which has a spacious master suite, and two other bedrooms. Harriett led us through the master suite (remodeled master bath, his and hers closets) and then into the first of the other bedrooms, which, she said, was the larger of the two.

"This one will be the guest room," Jenna said. We followed Harriett back into the hallway and to the doorway of the third bedroom.

"This one is smaller," she said as she entered the room. "You could use it as another guest bedroom, or as a study. It has a nice view of that big oak tree in the backyard, where a squirrel family lives."

Jenna had looked at me, smiled, put her arm through mine, and we headed for the stairway, leaving Harriett the realtor all alone in Hope's room.

The day before we moved out of our Edina house, Jenna found me in the basement, unplugging the electric water heater. She was carrying a piece of paper from a yellow legal pad. She smiled and handed it to me. On it, she'd written, "Thank you for helping our family, Edward. We are all right now. If you get this note, please let us know that you are, too. Love, Jack and Jenna Tanner." She had listed our new Ann Arbor address and my cell phone number.

I knew what Jenna wanted to do with her note. She followed me upstairs and I located an empty wine bottle in the kitchen trash basket, the kind with a screw top. I rolled up the note, put it inside the bottle, and screwed on the top. Then we went into the garage, got into our car, drove to downtown Minneapolis, and turned onto a concrete bridge over the Mississippi River connecting the mainland with Nicollet Island.

I pulled over and put on the emergency flashers. It was midafternoon, and there was no traffic on the bridge because there is not much to do on Nicollet Island. We got out and went to the railing. Jenna, who was holding the bottle, looked at me, the wind blowing her hair, and dropped it down into the river. It disappeared beneath the surface, then bobbed up and swirled around, trapped in an eddy. After a moment, the current took it and carried it downstream. Jenna and I stood there at the railing, my arm around her shoulder, and watched until it disappeared around a bend. Then we got back into our car and drove home.

The Mississippi originates in Lake Itasca in northern Minnesota and flows 2,350 miles south through the center of the continent to the Gulf of Mexico. Of course, I didn't expect that Edward Hollingsworth, if that is his real name, would ever notice the glint of sunlight on glass while trolling for billfish out in the Gulf Stream. But I like to think that he would not have to find that bottle with Jenna's note in it to know that the Tanner family really will be all right now.